RUTHLESS

Men who can't be tamed...or so they think!

If you love strong, commanding men,
you'll love this miniseries.
Meet the guy who breaks the rules to get
exactly what he wants, because he is...

HARD-EDGED & HANDSOME
He's the man who's impossible to resist...

RICH & RAKISH
He's got everything—and needs nobody...
Until he meets one woman...

He's RUTHLESS!
In his pursuit of passion; in his world
the winner takes all!

Brought to you by your favorite
Harlequin Presents® authors!

Carol Marinelli

WANTED: MISTRESS AND MOTHER

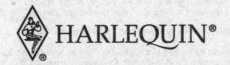

TORONTO • NEW YORK • LONDON
AMSTERDAM • PARIS • SYDNEY • HAMBURG
STOCKHOLM • ATHENS • TOKYO • MILAN • MADRID
PRAGUE • WARSAW • BUDAPEST • AUCKLAND

ISBN-13: 978-0-373-12616-3
ISBN-10:   0-373-12616-6

WANTED: MISTRESS AND MOTHER

First North American Publication 2007.

www.eHarlequin.com

Printed in U.S.A.

All about the author...
Carol Marinelli

CAROL MARINELLI finds writing a bio rather like writing her New Year's resolutions. Oh, she'd love to say that since she wrote the last one, she now goes to the gym regularly and doesn't stop for coffee, cake and gossip afterward; that she's incredibly organized; and that she writes for a few productive hours a day after tidying her immaculate house and taking a brisk walk with the dog.

The reality is Carol spends an inordinate amount of time daydreaming about dark, brooding men and exotic places (research), which doesn't leave too much time for the gym, housework or anything that comes in between. And her most productive writing hours happen to be in the middle of the night, which leaves her in a constant state of bewildered exhaustion.

Originally from England, Carol now lives in Melbourne, Australia. She adores going back to the U.K. for a visit—actually, she adores going anywhere for a visit—and constantly (expensively) strives to overcome her fear of flying. She has three gorgeous children who are growing up so fast (too fast— they've just worked out that she lies about her age!) and keep her busy with a never-ending round of homework, sports and friends coming over.

A nurse and a writer, Carol loves the fast-paced, busy setting of a modern hospital, but every now and then admits it's bliss to escape to the glamorous, alluring world of her heroes and heroines. A lot like her real life actually!

CHAPTER ONE

INAPPROPRIATE.

It was the first word that sprang to mind as dark, clearly irritated eyes swung round to face her, black eyes that stared down at Matilda, scrutinising her face unashamedly, making her acutely aware of her—for once—expertly made-up face. The vivid pink lipstick the beautician had insisted on to add a splash of colour to her newly straightened ash blonde hair and porcelain complexion seemed to suddenly render her mouth immovable, as, rather than slowing down to assist, the man she had asked for directions had instead, after a brief angry glance, picked up speed and carried on walking.

Inappropriate, because generally when you stopped someone to ask for directions, especially in a hospital, you expected to be greeted with a courteous nod or smile, for the person to actually slow down, instead of striding ahead and glaring back at you with an angry question of their own.

'Where?'

Even though he uttered just a single word, the thick, clipped accent told Matilda that English wasn't this man's first language. Matilda's annoyance at this response was doused a touch. Perhaps he was in the hospital to visit a sick relative, had just flown in to Australia from… In that split second her mind worked rapidly, trying to place him—his appearance was Mediterranean, Spanish or Greek perhaps, or maybe…

'Where is it you want to go?' he barked, finally deigning to slow down a fraction, the few extra words allowing Matilda to place his strong accent—he was Italian!

'I wanted to know how to find the function room,' she said slowly, repeating the question she had already asked, berating her luck that the only person walking through the maze of the hospital administration corridors spoke little English. That the tall, imposing man she had had to resort to for directions was blatantly annoyed at the intrusion. 'I'm trying to get there for the opening of the hospital garden. I'm supposed to be there in…' She glanced down at her watch and let out a sigh of exasperation. 'Actually, I was supposed to be there five minutes ago.'

'*Merda!*' As he glanced at his watch the curse that escaped his lips, though in Italian, wasn't, Matilda assumed, particularly complimentary, and abruptly stepping back she gave a wide-eyed look, before turning smartly on her heel and heading off to find her own way. He'd made it exceptionally clear that her request for assistance had been intrusive but now he was being downright rude. She certainly wasn't going to stand around and wait for the translation—she'd find the blessed function room on her own!

'I'm sorry.' He caught up with her in two long strides,

but Matilda marched on, this angry package of testosterone the very last thing she needed this morning.

'No, I'm sorry to have disturbed you,' Matilda called back over her shoulder, pushing the button—any button—on the lift and hoping to get the hell out of there. 'You're clearly busy.'

'I was cursing myself, not you.' He gave a tiny grimace, shrugged very wide shoulders in apology, which sweetened the explanation somewhat, and Matilda made a mental correction. His English was, in fact, excellent. It was just his accent that was incredibly strong—deep and heavy, and, Matilda reluctantly noted, incredibly sensual. 'I too am supposed to be at the garden opening, I completely forgot that they'd moved the time forward. My secretary has decided to take maternity leave.'

'How inconsiderate of her!' Matilda murmured under her breath, before stepping inside as the lift slid open.

'Pardon?'

Beating back a blush, Matilda stared fixedly ahead, unfortunately having to wait for him to press the button, as she was still none the wiser as to where the function room was.

'I didn't quite catch what you said,' he persisted.

'I didn't say anything,' Matilda lied, wishing the floor would open up and swallow her, or, at the very least, the blessed lift would get moving. There was something daunting about him, something incredibly confronting about his manner, his voice, his eyes; something very *inappropriate*.

There was that word again, only this time it had

nothing to do with his earlier rude response and everything to do with Matilda's as she watched dark, olive-
skinned hands punching in the floor number, revealing
a flash of an undoubtedly expensive gold watch under
heavy white cotton shirt cuffs. The scent of his bitter,
tangy aftershave was wafting over towards her in the
confined space and stinging into her nostrils as she reluctantly dragged in his supremely male scent. Stealing
a sideways glance, for the first time Matilda looked at
him properly and pieced together the features she had
so far only glimpsed.

He was astonishingly good-looking.

The internal admission jolted her—since her break-
up with Edward she hadn't so much as looked at a
man—certainly she hadn't looked at a man in *that*
way. The day she'd ended their relationship, like
bandit screens shooting up at the bank counter, it had
been as if her hormones had been switched off. Well,
perhaps not off, but even simmering would be an ex-
aggeration—the hormonal pot had been moved to the
edge of the tiniest gas ring and was being kept in a
state of tepid indifference: utterly jaded and completely immune.

Till now!

Never had she seen someone so exquisitely beautiful close up. It was as if some skilled photographer had
taken his magic wand and airbrushed the man from the
tip of his ebony hair right down to the soft leather of his
expensively shod toes. He seemed vaguely familiar—
and she tried over and over to place that swarthy, good-
looking face, sure that she must have seen him on the

TV screen because, if she'd witnessed him in the flesh, Matilda knew she would have remembered the occasion.

God, it was hot.

Fiddling with the neckline of her blouse, Matilda dragged her eyes away and willed the lift to move faster, only realising she'd been holding her breath when thankfully the doors slid open and she released it in a grateful sigh, as in a surprisingly gentlemanly move he stepped aside, gesturing for her to go first. But Matilda wished he'd been as rude on the fourth floor as he had been on the ground, wished, as she teetered along the carpeted floor of the administration wing in unfamiliar high heels, that she was walking behind instead of ahead of this menacing stranger, positive, absolutely positive that those black eyes were assessing her from a male perspective, excruciatingly aware of his eyes burning into her shoulders. She could almost feel the heat emanating from them as they dragged lower down to the rather too short second half of her smart, terribly new charcoal suit. And if legs could have blushed, then Matilda's were glowing as she felt his burning gaze on calves that were encased in the sheerest of stockings.

'Oh!' Staring at the notice-board, she bristled as he hovered over her shoulder, reading with growing indignation the words beneath the hastily drawn black arrow. 'The opening's been moved to the rooftop.'

'Which makes more sense,' he drawled, raising a curious, perfectly arched eyebrow at her obvious annoyance, before following the arrow to a different set of lifts. 'Given that it is the rooftop garden that's being officially opened today and not the function room.'

'Yes, but…' Swallowing her words, Matilda followed him along the corridor. The fact she'd been arguing for the last month for the speeches to be held in the garden and not in some bland function room had nothing to do with this man. Admin had decided that a brief champagne reception and speeches would be held here, followed by a smooth transition to the rooftop where Hugh Keller, CEO, would cut the ribbon.

The logistics of bundling more than a hundred people, in varying degrees of health, into a couple of lifts hadn't appeared to faze anyone except Matilda—until now.

But her irritation was short-lived, replaced almost immediately by the same flutter of nerves that had assailed her only moments before, her palms moist as she clenched her fingers into a fist, chewing nervously on her bottom lip as the lift doors again pinged open.

She didn't want to go in.

Didn't want that disquieting, claustrophobic feeling to assail her again. She almost turned and ran, her mind whirring for excuses—a quick dash to the loo perhaps, a phone call she simply had to make—but an impatient foot was tapping, fingers pressing the hold button, and given that she was already horribly late, Matilda had no choice.

Inadeguato.

As she stepped in hesitantly beside him, the word taunted him.

Inadeguato—to be feeling like this, to be *thinking* like this.

Dante could almost smell the arousal in the air as the doors closed and the lift jolted upwards. But it wasn't just her heady, feminine fragrance that reached him as he stood there, more the presence of her, the… He struggled for a word to describe his feelings for this delectable stranger, but even with two languages at his disposal, an attempt to sum up what he felt in a single word utterly failed him.

She was divine.

That was a start at least—pale blonde hair was sleeked back from an elfin face, vivid green eyes were surrounded by thick eyelashes and that awful lipstick she'd been wearing only moments ago had been nibbled away now—revealing dark, full red lips, lips that were almost too plump for her delicate face, and Dante found himself wondering if she'd had some work done on herself, for not a single line marred her pale features, her delicate, slightly snubbed nose absolutely in proportion to her petite features. She was certainly a woman who took care of herself. Her eyes were heavily made up, her hair fragranced and glossy—clearly the sort of woman who spent a lot of time in the beauty parlour. Perhaps a few jabs of collagen had plumped those delicious lips to kissable proportions, maybe a few units of Botox had smoothed the lines on her forehead, Dante thought as he found himself scrutinising her face more closely than he had a woman's in a long time.

A very long time.

He knew that it was wrong to be staring, *inadeguato* to be feeling this stir of lust for a woman he had never met, a woman whose name he didn't even know.

A woman who wasn't his wife.

The lift shuddered, and he saw her brow squiggle into

a frown, white teeth working her lips as the lift shuddered to a halt, and Dante's Botox theory went sailing out of the absent window!

'We're stuck!' Startled eyes turned to him as the lift jolted and shuddered to a halt, nervous fingers reaching urgently for the panel of buttons, but Dante was too quick for her, his hand closing around hers, pulling her finger back from hitting the panic button.

She felt as if she'd been branded—senses that had been on high alert since she'd first seen him screeched into overdrive, her own internal panic button ringing loudly now as his flesh closed around hers, the impact of his touch sending her into a spin, the dry, hot sensation of his fingers tightening around hers alarming her way more than the jolting lift.

'We are not stuck. This lift sometimes sticks here… see!' His fingers loosened from hers and as the lift shuddered back into life, for the first time Matilda noticed the gold band around his ring finger and it both disappointed and reassured her. The simple ring told her that this raw, testosterone-laden package of masculinity was already well and truly spoken for and suddenly Matilda felt foolish, not just for her rather pathetic reaction to the lift halting but for the intense feelings he had so easily evoked. She gave an apologetic grimace.

'Sorry. I'm just anxious to get there!'

'You seem tense.'

'Because I *am* tense,' Matilda admitted. The knowledge that he was married allowed her to let down her guard a touch now, sure in her own mind she had completely misread things, that the explosive reaction to him hadn't been in the least bit mutual, almost convincing herself that it was nerves about the opening that had set her on such a knife edge. Realising the ambiguity of her statement, Matilda elaborated. 'I hate this type of thing—' she started, but he jumped in, actually nodding in agreement.

'Me, too,' he said. 'There are maybe a hundred places I have to be this morning and instead I will be standing in some *stupido* garden on the top of a hospital roof, telling people how happy I am to be there…'

'*Stupid*?' Matilda's eyes narrowed at his response, anger bristling in her as he, albeit unwittingly, derided the months of painstaking work she had put into the garden they were heading up to. 'You think the garden is stupid?' Appalled, she swung around to confront him, realising he probably didn't know that she was the designer of the garden. But that wasn't the point—he had no idea who he was talking to, had spouted his arrogant opinion with no thought to who might hear it, no thought at all. But Dante was saved from her stinging response by the lift doors opening.

'Don't worry. Hopefully it won't take too long and we can quickly be out of there.' He rolled his eyes, probably expecting a sympathetic response, probably expecting a smooth departure from this meaningless, fleeting meeting, but Matilda was running behind him, tapping him smartly on the shoulder.

'Have you any idea the amount of work that goes into creating a garden like this?'

'No,' he answered rudely. 'But I know down to the last cent what it cost and, frankly, I can think of many more important things the hospital could have spent its money on.'

They were walking quickly, too quickly really for Matilda, but rage spurred her to keep up with him. 'People will get a lot of pleasure from this garden—sick people,' she added for effect, but clearly unmoved he just shrugged.

'Maybe,' he admitted, 'but if I were ill, I'd far rather that the latest equipment was monitoring me than have the knowledge that a garden was awaiting, if I ever made it up there.'

'You're missing the point…'

'I didn't realise there was one,' he frowned. 'I'm merely expressing an opinion and, given that it's mostly my money that paid for this "reflective garden", I happen to think I am entitled to one.'

'Your money?'

'My firm's.' He nodded, revealing little but at least allowing Matilda to discount the movie-star theory! 'Initially I was opposed when I heard what the hospital intended spending the donation on, but then some novice put in such a ridiculously low tender, I decided to let it go ahead. No doubt the landscape firm is now declaring bankruptcy, but at the end of the day the hospital has its garden and I appear a man of the people.' All this was said in superior tones with a thick accent so that Matilda was a second or two behind the conversation, blinking angrily as each word was deciphered and finally hit its mark. 'Never look a gift pony in the mouth.'

'Horse,' she retorted as she followed this impossible, obnoxious man up the disabled ramp that she had had installed to replace the three concrete steps and opened the small door that led onto the rooftop. 'The saying is never look a gift horse…' Her words petered out, the anger that fizzed inside, the nerves that had assailed her all morning fading as she stepped outside.

Outside into what she, Matilda Hamilton, had created.

The barren, concrete landscape of the hospital roof had become available when the helipad had been relocated to the newly built emergency department the previous year. The hospital had advertised in the newspaper, inviting tenders to transform the nondescript area into a retreat for patients, staff and relatives. A landscape designer by trade, most of her work to that point had been courtesy of her fiancé, Edward—a prominent real estate agent whose wealthy clients were only too happy to part with generous sums of money in order to bolster their properties prior to sale, or to transform Nana's neglected garden into a small oasis prior to an executor's auction. But as their relationship had steadily deteriorated, Matilda's desire to make it on her own had steadily increased. Despite Edwards's negativity and scorn, she'd registered a business name and duly made an appointment to take measurements of the rooftop and start her plans. Though she hadn't expected to make it past the first round, the second she had stepped onto the roof, excitement had taken over. It was as if she could *see* how it should be, could envision this dry, bland area transformed—endless potted trees supplying wind breaks and shade decorated with fairy lights to make it magical at night, cobbled paths where patients could meander and find their own space for reflection, mosaic tables filled with colour, messages of hope and inspiration adorning them like the stained-glass windows of a church where families could sit and share a coffee.

And water features!

Matilda's signature pieces were definitely in the plural—the gentle sound of running water audible at every turn, blocking out the hum of traffic or nearby people to enable peace or a private conversation. Hugh Keller had listened as she'd painted her vision with words, her hands flailing like windmills as she'd invited him into her mind's eye, described in minute detail the image she could so clearly see—a centre piece of water jets, shooting from the ground at various, random intervals, catching the sun and the colour from the garden—a centre piece where the elderly could sit and watch and children could play. And now that vision was finally a reality. In just a few moments' time, when Hugh cut the ribbon, the water features would be turned on and the garden declared open for all to enjoy!

'Matilda!' From all angles her name was being called and Matilda was glad for her momentary popularity—glad for the excuse to slip away from the man she'd walked in with. Not that he'd notice, Matilda thought, accepting congratulations and a welcome glass of champagne, but cross with herself that on this, perhaps the most important day of her life, a day when she should be making contacts, focusing on her achievement, instead she was recalling the brief encounter that had literally left her breathless, her mind drifting from the vitally important to the completely irrelevant.

He'd been nothing but rude, Matilda reminded herself firmly, smiling as Hugh waved through the crowd and made his way over towards her.

Very rude, Matilda reiterated to herself—good-looking he may be, impossibly sexy even, but he was obnoxious and—

'Hi, Hugh.' Matilda kissed the elderly gentleman on the cheek and dragged her mind back to the important event that was taking place. She listened intently as Hugh briefed her on the order of the speeches and part she would take in the day's events, but somewhere between Hugh reminding her to thank the mayor and the various sponsors Matilda's mind wandered, along with her eyes—coming to rest on that haughty profile that had both inflamed and enraged her since the moment of impact. Watching a man who stood a foot above a dignified crowd, engaged in conversation yet somehow remaining aloof, somehow standing apart from the rest.

And maybe he sensed he was being watched, perhaps it was her longing that made him turn around, but suddenly he was looking at her, making her feel just as he had a few moments ago in the lift, plunging her back to sample again those giddy, confusing sensations he somehow triggered. Suddenly her ability to concentrate on what Hugh was saying was reduced to ADHD proportions, the chatter in the garden fading into a distant hum as he blatantly held her gaze, just stared directly back at her as with cheeks darkening she boldly did the same. Although the sensible part of her mind was telling her to terminate things, to tear her eyes away, turn her back on him, halt this here and now, somehow she switched her internal remote to mute, somehow she tuned out the warnings and focused instead on the delicious picture.

'Once things calm down, hopefully we can discuss it.' Someone inadvertently knocking her elbow had Matilda snapping back to attention, but way too late to even attempt a recovery, Matilda realised as Hugh gave her a concerned look. 'Are you OK?'

'I'm so sorry, Hugh.' Reaching for her mental remote control, Matilda raised the volume, glanced at the gold band on the stranger's ring finger and, pointedly turning her back, flashed a genuinely apologetic smile. 'I really am. I completely missed that last bit of what you said. I'm a bundle of nerves at the moment, checking out that everything's looking OK…'

'Everything's looking wonderful, Matilda,' Hugh soothed, making her feel even guiltier! 'You've done an amazing job. I can't believe the transformation—just a bare old helipad and rooftop and now it's this oasis. Everyone who's been up here, from porters to consultants, has raved about it. I'm just glad it's finally going to be open for the people who really deserve to enjoy it: the patients and relatives.'

'Me, too.' Matilda smiled. 'So, what was it you wanted to discuss, Hugh?'

'A job.' Hugh smiled. 'Though I hear you're rather in demand these days.'

'Only thanks to you,' Matilda admitted. 'What sort of job?'

But it was Hugh who was distracted now, smiling at the mayor who was making his way towards them.

'Perhaps we could talk after the speeches—when things have calmed down a bit.'

'Of course.' Matilda nodded. 'I'll look forward to it!' More than Hugh knew. The thought of giving a speech— of facing this crowd, no matter how friendly—had filled her with dread for weeks now. The *business* side of running a business was really not her forte, but she'd done her best to look the part: had been to the beautician's and had her hair and make-up done—her hair today was neatly put up instead of thrown into a ponytail, expensive foundation replacing the usual slick of sun block and mascara. And the shorts, T-shirts and beloved Blundstone boots, which were her usual fare, had been replaced with a snappy little suit and painfully high heels. As the dreaded speeches started, Matilda stood with mounting heart rate and a very fixed smile, listening in suicidal despair as all her carefully thought-out lines and supposedly random thoughts were one by one used by the speakers that came before her. Tossing the little cards she had so carefully prepared into her—*new*—handbag, Matilda took to the microphone, smile firmly in place as Hugh adjusted it to her rather small height and the PA system shrieked in protest. Staring back at the mixture of curious and bored faces, only one really captured her, and she awaited his reaction—wondered how he would respond when he realised who he had insulted. But he wasn't even looking—his attention held by some ravishing brunette who was blatantly flirting with him. Flicking her eyes away, Matilda embarked on the first speech in her adult life, carefully thanking the people Hugh had mentioned before taking a deep breath and dragging in the heady fragrance of springtime and, as she always did, drawing strength from it.

'When I first met Hugh to discuss the garden, it was very clear that the hospital wanted a place that would provide respite,' Matilda started. 'A place where people could come and find if not peace then somewhere where they could gather their thoughts or even just take a breath that didn't smell of hospitals.' A few knowing nods from the crowd told her she was on the right track. 'With the help of many, many people, I think we've been able to provide that. Hospitals can be stressful places, not just for the patients and relatives but for the staff also, and my aim when I took on this job was to create an area void of signs and directions and overhead loud-speakers, a place where people could forget for a little while all that was going on beneath them, and hopefully that's been achieved.'

There were probably a million and one other things she could have said, no doubt someone else who needed to be thanked, but glancing out beyond the crowd, seeing the garden that had lived only in her mind's eye alive and vibrant, Matilda decided it was time to let Mother Nature speak for herself, to wrap up the speeches and let the crowd explore the haven she had tried so hard to create. She summed up with one heartfelt word.

'Enjoy!'

As Hugh cut the ribbon and the water jets danced into life, thin ribbons of water leaping into the air and catching the sunlight, Matilda felt a surge of pride at the oohs of the crowd and the excited shrieks of the children, doing just as she had intended: getting thoroughly wet and laughing as they did so. Only there was one child that didn't join in with the giggling and running, one little toddler who stood perfectly still, staring transfixed at the jets of water with huge solemn eyes, blonde curls framing her face. For some reason Matilda found herself staring, found herself almost willing the little girl to run and dance with the others, to see expression in that little frozen face.

'It's pretty, isn't it?' Crouching down beside her, Matilda held one of her hands out, breaking the stream of one of the jets, the cool water running through her fingers. 'You can touch it,' Matilda said, watching as slowly, almost fearfully a little fat hand joined Matilda's. A glimmer of a smile shivered on the little girl's lips, those solemn eyes glittering now as she joined in with the simple pleasure. As she saw Hugh coming over, Matilda found herself strangely reluctant to leave the child, sure that with just another few moments she could have had her running and dancing with the rest of the children.

'My granddaughter, Alex,' Hugh introduced them, crouching down also, but his presence went unnoted by Alex, her attention focused on the water running through her hands. 'She seems to like you.'

'She's adorable.' Matilda smiled, but it wavered on her lips, questions starting to form in her mind as the little girl still just stood there, not moving, not acknowledging the other children or her grandfather, just utterly, utterly lost in her own little world. 'How old is she?'

'Two,' Hugh said standing up, and pulling out a handkerchief, dabbing at his forehead for a moment.

'Are you OK,' Matilda checked, concerned at the slightly grey tinge to his face.

'I'll be fine,' Hugh replied. 'I've just been a bit off colour recently. She's two,' he continued, clearly wanting to change the subject. 'It was as actually Alex that I was hoping to talk to you about.'

'I thought it was a job…' Her voice trailed off, both of their gazes drifting towards the little girl, still standing there motionless. But her face was lit up with a huge smile, utterly entranced at the sight before her though still she didn't join in, she still stood apart, and with a stab of regret Matilda almost guessed what was coming next.

'She's been having some problems,' Hugh said, his voice thick with emotion. 'She was involved in a car accident over a year ago and though initially she appeared unharmed, gradually she's regressed, just re-treated really. She has the most appalling tantrums and outbursts followed by days of silence—the doctors are starting to say that she may be autistic. My wife Katrina and I are frantic…'

'Naturally.' Matilda gave a sympathetic smile, gen-uinely sorry to hear all Hugh was going through. He was a kind, gentle, friendly man, and even though they'd chatted at length over the last few months, he'd never given so much of a hint as to the problems in his personal life. But, then again, Matilda thought with a sigh, neither had she.

'I told my son-in-law last night that my wife and I would like to do this for Alex as a gift. There's a small gated area at the back of his property that I'm sure would be perfect for something like this—not on such a grand scale, of course, just somewhere that doesn't have rocks and walls and a pool…'

'Somewhere safe,' Matilda volunteered.

'Exactly.' Hugh gave a relieved nod. 'Somewhere she can't fall and hurt herself, somewhere she can run around unhindered or just sit and look at something beautiful. Look, I know you're booked up solidly for the next few months, but if one of the jobs gets cancelled could you bear me in mind? I hate to put pressure on you, Matilda, but I saw the joy in the children's faces when they saw the garden today. And if it can help Alex…' His voice trailed off and Matilda knew he wasn't attempting to gain her sympathy, Hugh would never do that. 'My son-in-law thinks that it's just a waste of time, that it isn't gong to help a bit, but at the very least Alex would have a garden that's safe and gives her some pleasure. I'm sure I'll be able to talk him around. At the end of the day he adores Alex—he'd do anything to help her.'

Matilda didn't know what to say—her diary was fill to burst with smart mews townhouses all wanting the inevitable low-maintenance, high-impact garden—but here was the man who had given her the head start, given her this opportunity. And more importantly, Matilda thought, her eyes lingering on Alex, here was a little girl who deserved all the help she could get. Her mind was working overtime—she could almost see the lazy couple of weeks' holiday she'd had planned before plunging into her next job slipping away out of her grasp as she took a deep breath and gave a small smile.

'Hugh, I'd need to get some details and then I'd need to actually see the site before I commit, but I have a couple of weeks off before I start on my next job, and I'm on pretty good terms with a few people. If I called in a few favours maybe I could do it for you. Where does Alex live?'

'Mount Eliza.' Hugh saw her give a small grimace. It had nothing to do with the location—Mount Eliza was a stunning, exclusive location overlooking Port Phillip Bay—but the distance from the city meant that it would cut down Matilda's working day considerably. 'It was their holiday residence before the accident, but since then… Look, would it make it easier if you stayed there? There's plenty of room.'

'I don't think I'd be able to do it otherwise,' Matilda admitted. 'I'll have workers arriving at the crack of dawn and I'm going to need to be there to meet them and show them what I need done.'

'It won't be a problem,' Hugh assured her, and after a moment of deep thought Matilda gave a small nod and then followed it up with a more definite one.

'I'd be happy to do it.'

'You mean it?'

'Of course.' Matilda smiled more widely now, Hugh's obvious delight making her spur-of-the-moment choice easily the right one.

'I feel awful that you won't even get a break.'

'That's what being in business is all about apparently.' Matilda shrugged her shoulders. 'Anyway, I'm sure lean times will come—it won't stay spring for ever and anyway it mightn't be such a big job. I'd be glad to do it, Hugh, but I do need a few more details from you, and you need to get your son-in-law's permission—I can't go digging up his land and planting things if he doesn't want me there in the first place. Now, I need to know the size of the land, any existing structures…' Matilda gave in as yet another group was making its way over, and Hugh's secretary tapped him on the arm to take an important phone call.

'It's impossible to discuss it here.' Hugh gave an apologetic smile. 'And it's probably inappropriate. You should be enjoying the celebrations—perhaps we could do it over dinner tonight. I'll see if my son-in-law can come along—I'm sure once he hears first hand about it he'll be more enthusiastic. Actually, there he is—I'll go and run it by him now.'

'Good idea,' Matilda agreed, crouching down again to play with Alex, her head turning to where Hugh was waving. But the smile died on her face as again she found herself staring at the man who had taken up so much of her mental energy today—watching as he walked around the water feature, a frown on his face as he watched her interact with his daughter.

'Dante!' Clearly not picking up on the tension, Hugh called him over, but Dante didn't acknowledge either of them, his haughty expression only softening when Matilda stepped back, his features softer now as he eyed his daughter. Matilda felt a curious lump swell in her throat as, with infinite tenderness, he knelt down beside Alex, something welling within as he spoke gently to his daughter.

'I'll have a word with Dante and make a booking for

tonight, then,' Hugh checked hopefully—too pleased to notice Matilda's stunned expression. The most she could manage was the briefest of nods as realisation started to dawn.

She'd barely managed two minutes in the lift with him and now she was about to be his house guest!

He's a husband and father, Matilda reminded herself firmly, calming herself down a touch, almost convincing herself she'd imagined the undercurrents that had sizzled between them.

And even if she hadn't misread things, even if there was an attraction between them, he was a married man and she wouldn't forget it for a single moment!

CHAPTER TWO

SHE didn't want to do this.

Walking towards the restaurant, Matilda was tempted to turn on her stilleto heels and run. She *hated* with a passion the formalities that preceded a garden make-over, looking at plans, talking figures, time-frames—and the fact she hadn't even seen the garden made this meeting a complete time-waster. But, Matilda was quickly realizing, this type of thing was becoming more and more frequent. As her business took off, gone were the days where she rolled up on a doorstep in her beloved Blundstone boots, accepted a coffee if she was lucky enough to be offered one and drew a comprehensive sketch of her plans for the owners, along with a quote for her services—only to spend the next few days chewing her nails and wondering if they'd call, worrying if perhaps she'd charged too much or, worse, seriously underquoted and would have to make up the difference herself.

Now her initial meetings took place in people's offices or restaurants, and even if she *was* lucky enough to be invited into their homes, Matilda had quickly learnt that her new clientele expected a smart, efficient professional for that first important encounter.

But it wasn't just the formalities that were causing butterflies this evening. Ducking into the shadowy retreat of a large pillar beside the restaurant, Matilda stopped for a moment, rummaged in her bag and pulled out a small mirror. She touched up her lipstick and fiddled with her hair for a second, acknowledging the *real* reason for anxiety tonight.

Facing Dante.

Even his name made her stomach ball into a knot of tension. She'd wanted him to remain nameless—for that brief, scorching but utterly one-sided encounter to be left at that—to somehow push him to the back of her mind and completely forget about him.

And now she was going to be working for him!

Maybe this dinner was *exactly* what she needed, Matilda consoled herself, peeling herself from the pillar ready to walk the short distance that remained to the restaurant. Maybe a night in his arrogant, obnoxious, pompous company would purge whatever it was that had coursed through her system since she'd laid eyes on him, and anyway, Matilda reassured herself, Hugh was going to be there, too.

An impressive silver car pulling up at the restaurant caught Matilda's attention and as the driver walked around and opened the rear door in a feat of self-preservation she found herself stepping back into the shadows, watching as the dignified figure of Dante stepped out—she had utterly no desire to enter the restaurant with him and attempt small talk until she had the reassuring company of Hugh.

He really was stunning, Matilda sighed, feeling slightly voyeuristic as she watched him walk. Clearly she wasn't the only one who thought so. From the second he'd stepped out of the car, heads had turned, a few people halting their progress to watch as if it were some celebrity arriving on the red carpet. But just as the driver was about to close the car door, just as the doorman greeted him, a piercing shriek emanating from the car had every head turning.

Especially Dante's.

Even from here she could see the tension etched in his face as he walked back towards the car, from where an anxious young woman appeared, holding the furious, livid, rigid body of his daughter. Grateful for the shadows, Matilda watched with something akin to horror as, oblivious to the gathering crowd, he took the terrified child from the woman and attempted to soothe her, holding her angry, unyielding body against his, talking to her in low, soothing tones, capturing her tiny wrists as she attempted to gouge him, her little teeth like those of a feral animal. Matilda had never seen such anger, never witnessed such a paroxysm of rage, could scarcely comprehend that it could come from someone so small.

'That child needs a good smack, if you ask me,' an elderly lady volunteered, even though no one had asked her. Matilda had to swallow down a smart reply, surprising herself at her own anger over such a thoughtless comment—tempted now to step out from the shadows and offer her support, to see if there was anything she could do to help. But almost as soon as it had started it was over. The fight that had fuelled Alex left her, her little body almost slumping in defeat, the shrieks replaced by quiet, shuddering sobs, which were so pain-filled they were almost harder to bear. After a moment more of tender comfort, with a final nod Dante handed her back to the woman, his taut, strained face taking in every detail as the duo headed for the car, before, without deigning to give the crowd a glance, he headed into the restaurant.

Pushing open the door, though shaken from what she had just witnessed, Matilda attempted assurance as her eyes worked the restaurant, her smile ready for Hugh, but as the waiter took her name and guided her towards the table, she was again tempted to turn tail and run.

It was definitely a table for two—but instead of the teddy bear proportions of Hugh, instead of his beaming red face smiling to greet her, she was met by the austere face of Dante, his tall muscular frame standing as she approached, his face expressionless as she crossed the room. If Matilda hadn't witnessed it herself, she'd never have believed what he'd just been through, for nothing in his stance indicated the hellish encounter of only moments before.

In her peripheral vision she was aware of heads turning, but definitely not towards her, could hear flickers of conversation as she walked towards him.

'Is he famous…?'

'He looks familiar…'

He looked familiar because he was perfection—a man that normally glowered from the centre of the glossiest of glossy magazines, a man who should be dressed in nothing more than a ten-thousand-dollar watch or in the driver's seat of a luxury convertible.

He certainly wasn't the type of man that Matilda was used to dining with…

And certainly not alone.

Please, Matilda silently begged, please, let a waiter appear, breathlessly dragging a table over, and preferably, another waiter, too, to hastily turn those two table settings into three. Please, please, let it not be how it looked.

'Matilda.' His manners were perfect, waiting till she was seated before sitting down himself, patiently waiting as she gave her drink order to the waiter. She was pathetically grateful that she'd chosen to walk to the restaurant—no mean feat in her fabulous new shoes, but there was no chance of a punctual taxi this time on a Friday evening, and by the time she'd parked she could have been here anyway.

Good choice.

Good, because she could now order a gin and tonic, and hopefully douse some of the rowdier butterflies that were dancing in her stomach

'Hugh sends his apologies.' Dante gave her a very on-off smile as Matilda frowned. The Hugh she knew would be the last person to have bailed—no matter how important the diversion. After all, he'd practically begged her to do the garden.

'He had a headache after the opening. He didn't look well, so I walked him back to his office where he had…' Dante snapped his fingers, clearly trying to locate his word

of choice. 'He had a small turn,' he said finally, as
Matilda's expression changed from a frown to one of
horror.

'Oh, my goodness…'

'He's OK,' Dante said quickly. 'His blood pressure
has been very high for the past few months, the doctors
have had him on several different combinations of
tablets to try to lower it, but it would seem the one
they'd recently given him has brought it down too low—
that's why he had a small collapse. Luckily we were in
the hospital when it happened—all I had to do was pick
up the phone.'

'You're not a doctor, then.'

Dante gave a slightly startled look. 'Heavens, no.
What on earth gave you that impression?'

'I don't know,' Matilda shrugged. 'You seemed to
know your way around the hospital…'

'I've spent rather too much time there,' Dante said,
and Matilda could only assume he was talking about
Alex. But he revealed absolutely nothing, promptly di-
verting the subject from himself back to Hugh. 'He's
resting at home now, but naturally he wasn't well
enough to come out. Hugh feels terrible to have let you
down after you were kind enough to accommodate him
at such short notice. I tried many times to contact you
on your mobile…'

'My phone isn't on,' Matilda said, flustered. 'I never
thought to check.'

Fool, Matilda raged to herself. He'd been frantically
trying to cancel, to put her off, and because her blessed
phone hadn't been turned on, Dante had been forced to

show up and babysit her when he hadn't even wanted her to do the garden in the first place, when clearly he wanted to be at home with his daughter.

Taking a grateful sip of her drink, Matilda eyed the proffered menu, her face burning in uncomfortable embarrassment, utterly aware that here with her was the last place Dante either wanted or needed to be tonight.

'I've agreed to the garden.' Dante broke the difficult silence. 'Hugh said that I had to see you to give my consent. Do I need to sign anything?'

'It isn't a child custody battle.' Matilda looked up and for the first time since she'd joined him at the table actually managed to look him in the eye. 'I don't need your written consent or anything. I just wanted to be sure that you were happy for me to work on your garden.'

'It's not a problem,' Dante said, which was a long way from happy.

'I have brought along the plans for you to look at— I've highlighted the area Hugh discussed with you.' Glancing up, Dante nodded to the waiter who had approached, giving him permission to speak.

'Are you ready to order, sir?'

The waiter hovered as Dante turned to Matilda, but she shook her head.

'Could you give us a minute?' Dante asked and the waiter melted away. Clearly assuming she was out of her depth, he proceeded to walk her through the menu. 'I will be having my usual gnocchi, but I hear that the Tasmanian salmon is excellent here—it's wild—'

'I'm sure it's divine,' Matilda interrupted. 'I do know

how to read a menu, Dante. And there's really no need to go through the charade of a meal…'

'Charade?'

Matilda resisted rolling her eyes.

'The pretence,' she explained, but Dante interrupted her.

'I do know how to speak English, Matilda.' He flashed her a tight smile. 'Why do you call it a charade?'

'Because we both know that you don't want the garden, that you've probably only agreed because Hugh's unwell…' He opened his mouth to interrupt but Matilda spoke on. 'You tried to contact me to cancel. I'm sorry, I never thought to check my phone. So why don't I save up both an uncomfortable evening? We can drink up, I'll take the plans and ring tomorrow to arrange a convenient time to come and look at your property. There's really no need to make a meal out of it—if you'll excuse the pun.'

'The pun?'

'The pun.' Matilda bristled then rolled her eyes. 'It's a saying—let's not make a meal out of things, as in let's not make a big deal out of it, but given that we were about to *have* a meal…'

'You made a pun.'

God, why was the English language so complicated at times?

'I did.' Matilda smiled brightly, but it didn't reach her eyes.

'So you don't want to eat?'

'I don't want to waste your time.' Matilda swallowed hard, not sure whether to broach the subject that was undoubtedly on both their minds. 'I saw you arrive…'

Taking a gulp of her drink, Matilda waited, waited for his face to colour a touch, for him to admit to the problem he had clearly faced by being here, but again Dante revealed nothing, just left her to stew a moment longer in a very uncomfortable silence. 'Alex seemed very…upset; so I'm sure that dinner is the last thing you need tonight.'

'Alex is often upset,' Dante responded in a matter-of-fact voice, which did nothing to reassure her. 'And given it is already after eight and I haven't stopped all day, dinner is exactly what I need now.' He snapped his fingers for the waiter and barked his short order. 'My usual.'

'Certainly, and, madam…?'

Matilda faltered, desperate to go yet wanting to stay all the same.

'*Madam*?' Dante smiled tightly, making her feel like one.

'The salmon for me. *Please*,' she added pointedly as the waiter took her menu. Then, remembering that as uncomfortable as she might feel, this was, in fact, a business dinner, Matilda attempted an apology. 'I'm sorry if I was rude before,' she said once the waiter had left. 'It's just I got the impression from Hugh that this meeting tonight was the last thing you wanted.'

'Funny, that.' Dante took a long sip of his drink before continuing, 'I got the same impression from Hugh, too…' He smiled at her obvious confusion.

'Why would you think that?' Matilda asked.

'Hugh gave me strict orders not to upset you.' He flashed a very bewitching grin and Matilda found herself smiling back, not so much in response to his smile, more at the mental picture of *anyone* giving this man strict orders about anything. 'He told me that you were booked up months ahead, and that you'd agree to come in and do this job during your annual leave.'

'Yes…' Matilda admitted, 'but—'

'He also told me that you were doing this as a favour because he'd backed your tender, that you felt obliged—'

'Not all obligations are bad,' Matilda broke in, rather more forcibly this time. 'I *did* agree to work on your garden during my holiday and, yes, I *did* feel a certain obligation to Hugh because of the faith he showed in my proposal for the hospital garden, but I can assure you that I was more than happy to do the work.'

'Happy?' Dante gave a disbelieving smile.

'Yes, happy.' Matilda nodded. 'I happen to like my work, Dante. I just want to make sure that you're fine with me being there.'

'I'm fine with it.' Dante gave a short nod.

'Because Hugh's sick?'

'Does it really matter?'

Matilda thought for a moment before answering. 'It does to me,' she said finally. 'And whether it's ego or neurosis, I'd like to think that when I pour my heart and soul into a job at least my efforts will be appreciated. If you and your wife are only doing this to pacify Hugh, then you're doing it for the wrong reasons. To make it effective, I'm going to need a lot of input as to your daughter's likes and dislikes. It needs to be a reflection of her and I'd like to think that it's going to be a place the whole family can enjoy.'

'Fair enough.' Dante gave a tight shrug. 'I admit I do not believe that a garden, however special, can help my daughter, but I am willing to give it a try—I've tried everything else after all…'

'I clearly explained to Hugh that this garden isn't going to be a magical cure for your daughter's problems—it might bring her some peace, some respite, a safe place that could help soothe her…'

'If that were the case…' Dante said slowly and for the first time since she had met him his voice wasn't superior or scathing but distant. Matilda felt a shiver run through her as she heard the pain behind his carefully chosen words. 'It would be more than worth it.'

'Look.' Her voice was softer now. 'Why don't I take the plans and have a look? Then maybe on Sunday I could speak with your wife about Alex…'

'My wife is dead.'

He didn't elaborate, didn't soften it with anything. His voice was clipped and measured, his expression devoid of emotion as he explained his situation, the pain she had witnessed just a second before when he'd spoken about his daughter gone now, as if a safety switch had been pushed, emotion switched off, plunging his features into unreadable darkness as she faltered an apology.

'I had no idea,' Matilda breathed. 'I'm so very sorry.'

He didn't shake his head, didn't wave his hand and say that she couldn't have known… just let her stew in her own embarrassment as their food arrived, raining salt and pepper on his gnocchi until Matilda could take it no more. Excusing herself, she fled to the loo and leaned over the basin, screwing her eyes closed as she relived the conversation.

'Damn, damn damn!' Cursing herself, she relived every insensitive word she'd uttered, then peeped her eyes open and closed them again as a loo flushed and she was forced to fiddle with her lipstick as a fellow diner gave her a curious glace as she washed her hands. Alone again, Matilda stared at her glittering eyes and flushed reflection in the massive gilt-edged mirror and willed her heart to slow down.

She'd apologise again, Matilda decided. She'd march straight out of the bathroom and say that she was sorry. No, she'd leave well alone—after all, she'd done nothing wrong. Of course she'd assumed his wife was alive. He had a child, he wore his wedding ring. She had nothing to apologise for.

So why had she fled? Why didn't she want to go back out there?

'Everything OK?' Dante checked as she slid back into her seat.

'Everything's fine,' Matilda attempted, then gave up on her false bravado and let out a long-held sigh. 'I'm just not very good at this type of thing.'

'What type of thing?'

'Business dinners.' Matilda gave a tight smile. 'Though I should be, given the number that I've been to.'

'I thought that your business was new.'

'It is.' Matilda nodded, taking a drink of her wine before elaborating. 'But my ex-fiancé was a real estate agent…'

'Ouch,' Dante said, and Matilda felt a rather disloyal smile to Edward twitch on her lips.

'He was very good,' Matilda said defensively. 'Incredibly good, actually. He has a real eye for what's needed to make a house sell well. It's thanks to Edward that I got started. If he was selling a deceased estate often it would be neglected, the gardens especially, and I'd come in…'

'And add several zeros to the asking price!' Dante said with a very dry edge, taking the positive spin out of Matilda's speech. She gave a rather glum nod.

'But it wasn't like that at first.'

Dante gave a tight smile. 'It never is.'

'So what do you do?' Matilda asked, chasing her rice with a fork as Dante shredded his bread and dipped it in a side dish of oil and balsamic vinegar, wishing as she always did when she was out that she'd had what he'd had!

'I'm a barrister. My specialty is criminal defence.' Matilda's fork frozen over her fish spoke volumes. 'Ouch!' he offered, when Matilda didn't say anything.

'Double ouch.' Matilda gave a small, tight smile as reality struck. 'Now you come to mention it, I think I know your name…' Matilda took another slug of wine as newspaper reports flashed into her mind, as a lazy Sunday afternoon spent reading the colour supplements a few months ago took on an entirely new meaning. 'Dante Costello—you defended that guy who—'

'Probably,' Dante shrugged.

'But—'

'I defend the indefensible.' Dante was unmoved by her obvious discomfort. 'And I usually win.'

'And I suppose your donation to the hospital was an attempt to soften your rather brutal image.'

'You suppose correctly.' Dante nodded, only this time

his arrogance didn't annoy her—in fact, his rather brutal honesty was surprisingly refreshing. 'I try to give back, sometimes with good intentions.' He gave another, rather elaborate, shrug. 'Other times because…'

'Because?' Matilda pushed, and Dante actually laughed.

'Exactly as you put it, Matilda, I attempt to soften my rather brutal image.' She liked the way he said her name. Somehow with his deep Italian voice, he made it sound beautiful, made a name that had until now always made her cringe sound somehow exotic. But more than that it was the first time she'd seen him laugh and the effect was amazing, seeing his bland, unfathomable face soften a touch, glimpsing his humour, a tiny peek at the man behind the man.

They ate in more amicable silence now, the mood more relaxed, and Matilda finally addressed the issue that they were, after all, there for.

'It would help if you could tell me a bit about Alex—her likes and dislikes.'

'She loves water,' Dante said without hesitation. 'She also…' He broke off with a shake of his head. 'It's nothing you can put in a garden.'

'Tell me,' Matilda said eagerly.

'Flour,' Dante said. 'She plays with dough and flour…'

'The textures are soothing,' Matilda said and watched as Dante blinked in surprise. 'I found that out when I was researching for the hospital garden. A lot of autistic children…' She winced at her insensitivity, recalled that it was only a tentative diagnosis and one that the family didn't want to hear. 'I'm so—'

'Please, don't apologise again,' Dante broke in with a distinct dry edge to his voice. 'It's becoming rather repetitive. Anyway,' he said as Matilda struggled for a suitable response, 'it is I who should apologise to you: I embarrassed you earlier when I told you about my wife. You can probably gather that I'm not very good at telling people. I tend to be blunt.' He gave a very taut smile and Matilda offered a rather watery one back, reluctant to say anything in the hope her silence might allow him to elaborate. For the first time since she'd met him, her instincts were right. She watched as he swallowed, watched as those dark eyes frowned over the table towards her, and she knew in that second that he was weighing her up, deciding whether or not to go on. Her hand convulsed around her knife and fork, scared to move, scared to do anything that might dissuade him, might break this fragile moment, not even blinking until Dante gave a short, almost imperceptible nod and spoke on.

'Fifteen months ago, I had a normal, healthy daughter. She was almost walking, she smiled she blew kisses, she waved, she was even starting to talk, and then she and my wife were involved in a car accident. Alex was strapped in her baby seat. It took two hours to extricate my wife and daughter from the car...' Matilda felt a shiver go through her as he delivered his speech and in that moment she understood him, understood the mask he wore, because he was speaking as he must work, discarding the pain, the brutal facts, the horrors that must surely haunt him. And stating mere facts— hellish, gut-wrenching facts that were delivered in perhaps the only way he could: the detached voice of a newsreader. 'Jasmine was unconscious, pronounced dead on arrival at hospital.' He took a sip of his drink, probably, Matilda guessed, to take a break from the emotive tale, rather than to moisten his lips. But other than that he appeared unmoved, and she could only hazard a guess at the torture he had been through, the sheer force of willpower and rigid self-control that enabled him to deliver this speech so dispassionately. 'At first Alex, apart from a few minor injures, appeared to have miraculously escaped relatively unscathed. She was kept in hospital for a couple of nights with bruising and for observation but she seemed fine…'

Dante frowned, his eyes narrowing as he looked across to where Matilda sat, but even though he was looking directly at her, Matilda knew he couldn't see her, that instead he was surveying a painful moment in time, and she sat patient and still as Dante took a moment to continue. 'But, saying that, I guess at the time I wasn't really paying much attention…' His voice trailed off again and this time Matilda did speak, took up this very fragile thread, wanting so very much to hear more, to know this man just a touch better.

'You must have had a lot on your mind,' Matilda volunteered gently, and after a beat of hesitation Dante nodded.

'I often wonder if I failed to notice something. I was just so grateful that Alex seemed OK and she really did appear to be, but a couple of months later—it was the twenty-second of September—she started screaming…' He registered Matilda's frown and gave a small wistful smile.. 'I remember the date because it would have been Jasmine's birthday. They were all difficult days, but that one in particular was…' He didn't elaborate, he didn't need to. 'I was getting ready to go to the cemetery, and it was as if Alex knew. When I say she was screaming, it wasn't a usual tantrum, she was *hysterio*, deranged. It took hours to calm her. We called a doctor, and he said she was picking up on my grief, that she would be fine, but even as he spoke, even as I tried to believe him, I knew this was not normal, that something was wrong. Unfortunately I was right.'

'It carried on?'

Dante nodded.

'Worse each time, terrible, unmitigated outbursts of rage, and there's no consoling her, but worse, far worse, is the withdrawal afterwards, her utter detachment. I spoke to endless doctors, Hugh was concerned, Katrina in denial…'

'Denial?'

'She refuses to admit there is a problem. So do I too at times, but I could not pretend things were OK and Katrina was starting to get…' he stopped himself then, took a sip of his drink before continuing. 'After a few months I took Alex home to Italy—I thought a change of environment might help. And, of course, it did help to have my family around me, but Hugh and Katrina were devastated,' Dante continued. 'They'd lost their daughter and now it seemed to them that I was taking away their granddaughter. But I had no choice and for a while Alex improved, but then suddenly, from nowhere, it all started again.'

'So you came back?'

'For now.' Dante shrugged. 'I am back in Australia to try and sort things out and make my decision. I have a major trial coming up in a week's time so I am still working, but I am not taking on any new cases. You see now why it seemed pointless to renovate the garden when I do not know if Alex will even be here to enjoy it. But I think that Hugh and Katrina are hoping if they can do something—*anything*—to improve things, there is more chance that I will stay.'

'And is there?' Matilda asked, surprised at how much his answer mattered to her. 'Is there a chance you might stay?'

'My family is in Italy,' Dante pointed out. 'I have two brothers and three sisters, all living near Rome. Alex would have her *nona*, *nono* and endless cousins to play with, I would have more family support, instead of relying on Katrina and Hugh, but…' He halted the conversation then, leaving her wanting to know more, wanting a deeper glimpse of him. Wondering what it was that kept him here, what it was that made him stay. But the subject was clearly closed. 'It cannot be about me,' Dante said instead, giving a tight shrug, and there was a finality to his words as he effectively ended the discussion. But Matilda, wanting more, attempted to carry it on.

'What about your work?'

'I am lucky.' He gave a dry smile. 'There is always someone getting into trouble, either here or in Italy— and being bilingual is a huge advantage. I can work in either country.'

'Doesn't it bother you?' Matilda asked, knowing that she was crossing a line, knowing the polite thing to do would be to leave well alone, but her curiosity was piqued, her delectable salmon forgotten, barely registering as the waiter filled her wine glass. 'Defending those sorts of people, I mean.'

'I believe in innocent until proven guilty.'

'So do I,' Matilda said, staring into that brooding emotionless face and wondering what, if anything, moved him. She'd never met anyone so confident in their own skin, so incredibly not out to impress. He clearly didn't give a damn what people thought of him; he completely dispensed with the usual social niceties and yet somehow he managed to wear it, somehow it worked. 'But you can't sit there and tell me that that guy who killed—'

'That guy,' Dante broke in, 'was proved innocent in a court of law.'

'I know.' Matilda nodded but it changed midway, her head shaking, incredulity sinking in. She certainly wasn't a legal eagle, but you'd have to live in a cupboard not to know about some of the cases Dante Costello handled. They were *Big*, in italics and with a capital B. And even *if* that man she had read about really had been innocent, surely some of the people Dante had defended really were guilty. His job was so far removed from hers as to be unfathomable, and bewildered, she stared back at him. 'Do you ever regret winning?'

'No.' Firmly he shook his head.

'Never?' Matilda asked, watching his lips tighten a touch, watching his eyes darken from dusk to midnight.

'Never,' Dante replied, his single word unequivocal. She felt a shiver, could almost see him in his robes and wig, could almost see that inscrutable face remaining unmoved, could see that full mouth curving into a sneer as he shredded seemingly irrefutable evidence. And anyone, everyone, would have left it there, would have conceded the argument, yet Matilda didn't, green eyes crashing into his, jade waves rolling onto unmovable black granite.

'I don't believe you.'

'Then you don't know what you're talking about.'

'I know I don't,' Matilda admitted. 'Yet I still don't believe you.'

And that should have been it. She should have got on with her meal, he should have resumed eating, made polite small talk to fill the appalling gap, but instead he pushed her now. As she reached for her fork he reached deep inside, his words stilling her, his hand seemingly clutching her heart. 'You've been proud of everything you've done.'

'Not everything,' Matilda tentatively admitted. 'But there's certainly nothing big league. Anyway, what's that got to do with it?'

'It has everything to do with it,' Dante said assuredly. 'We all have our dark secrets, we all have things that, given our time again, we would have done differently. The difference between Mr or Ms Average and my clients is that their personal lives, their most intimate regrets are up for public scrutiny. Words uttered in anger are played back to haunt them, a moment of reckless-ness a couple of years back suddenly relived for everyone to hear. It can be enough to cloud the most objective jury.'

'But surely, if they've done nothing wrong,' Matilda protested, 'they have nothing to fear.'

'Not if I do my job correctly,' Dante said. 'But not everyone's as good as me.' Matilda blinked at his lack of modesty, but Dante made no apology. 'I *have* to believe that my clients are innocent.'

She should have left it there, Matilda knew that, knew she had no chance against him, but she refused to be a pushover and refused to be swayed from her stance. She wasn't in the witness box after all, just an adult having an interesting conversation. There was no need to be intimidated. Taking a breath, she gave him a very tight smile. 'Even if they're clearly not?'

'Ah, Matilda.' He flashed her an equally false smile. 'You shouldn't believe all you read in the newspapers.'

'I don't,' Matilda flared. 'I'm just saying that there's no smoke without fire…' She winced at the cliché and began to make a more eloquent argument, but Dante got there first.

'There are no moments in your life that you'd dread coming out in court?'

'Of course not!'

'None at all?'

'None,' Matilda flushed. 'I certainly haven't done anything illegal, well, not really.'

'Not really?' Nothing in his expression changed, bar a tiny rise of one eyebrow.

'I thought we were here to talk about your garden,' she flared, but Dante just smiled.

'You were the one who questioned me about my work,' Dante pointed out. 'It's not my fault if you don't like the answer. So, come on, tell me, what did you do?'

'I've told you,' Matilda insisted. 'I've done *nothing* wrong. I'm sorry if you find that disappointing or boring.'

'I'm *never* disappointed,' Dante said, his eyes burning into her, staring at her so directly it made her squirm. 'And I know for a fact that you have your secret shame—everyone does.'

'OK,' Matilda breathed in indignation. 'But if you're expecting some dark, sordid story then you're going to be sorely disappointed. It's just a tiny, tiny thing that happened when I was a kid.'

'Clearly not that tiny,' Dante said, 'if you can still blush just thinking about it.'

'I'm not blushing,' Matilda flared, but she knew it was useless, could feel the sting of heat on her cheeks. But it wasn't the past that was making her blush, it was the present, the here and now, the presence of him, the feel of his eyes on her, the intimacy of revelation—any revelation.

'Tell me,' Dante said softly, dangerously, and it sounded like a dare. 'Tell me what happened.'

'I stole some chocolate when I was on school camp,' Matilda admitted. 'Everyone did,' she went on almost immediately.

'And you thought that you'd look an idiot if you didn't play along?'

'Something like that,' Matilda murmured, blushing furiously now, but with the shame and fear she had felt at the time, reliving again the pressure she had felt at that tender age to just blend in. She was surprised at the emotion such a distant memory could evoke.

'So, instead of standing up for yourself, you just went right along with it, even though you knew it was wrong.'

'I guess.'

'And that's the sum total of your depraved past?' Dante checked.

'That's it.' Matilda nodded. 'Sorry if I disappointed you.'

'You didn't.' Dante shook his head. 'I find you can learn a lot about a person if you listen to their childhood memories. Our responses don't change that much…'

'Rubbish,' Matilda scoffed. 'I was ten years old. If something like that happened now—'

'You'd do exactly the same,' Dante broke in. 'I'm not saying that you'd steal a bar of chocolate rather than draw attention to yourself, but you certainly don't like confrontation, do you?'

Shocked at his insight, all she could do was stare back at him.

'In fact,' Dante continued, 'you'd walk to the end of the earth to avoid it, steal a chocolate bar if it meant you could blend in, stay in a bad relationship to avoid a row…' As she opened her mouth to deny it, Dante spoke over her. 'Or, let's take tonight for an example, you ran to the toilet the moment you thought you had upset me.'

'Not quite that very moment.' Matilda rolled her eyes and gave a watery smile, realising she was beaten. 'I lasted two at least. But does anyone actually like confrontation?'

'I do,' Dante said. 'It's the best part of my job, making people confront their hidden truths.' He gave her the benefit of a very bewitching smile, which momentarily knocked her off guard. 'Though I guess if that's the worst you can come up with, you really would have no problem with being cross-examined.'

'I'd have no worries at all,' Matilda said confidently.

'You clearly know your own mind.'

'I do.' Matilda smiled back, happy things were under control.

'Then may I?'

'Excuse me?'

'Just for the sake of curiosity.' His smile was still in place. 'May I ask you some questions?'

'We're supposed to be talking about your garden.'

He handed her a rolled-up wad of paper. 'There are the plans, you can do whatever you wish—so that takes care of that.'

'But why?' Matilda asked.

'I enjoy convincing people.' Dante shrugged. 'And I believe you are far from convinced. All you have to do is answer some questions honestly.'

The dessert menu was being offered to her and Matilda hesitated before taking it. She had the plans, and clearly Dante was in no mood to discuss foliage or water features, so the sensible thing would be to decline. She'd eaten her main course, she'd stayed to be polite, there was absolutely no reason to prolong things, no reason at all—except for the fact that she wanted to stay.

Wanted to prolong this evening.

With a tiny shiver Matilda accepted the truth.

She wanted to play his dangerous game.

'They do a divine white chocolate and macadamia nut mousse,' Dante prompted, 'with hot raspberry sauce.'

'Sounds wonderful,' Matilda said, and as the waiter slipped silently away, her glittering eyes met Dante's. A frisson of excitement ran down her spine as she faced him, as this encounter moved onto another level, and not for the first time today she wondered what it was about Dante Costello that moved her so.

CHAPTER THREE

'YOU will answer me honestly?'

His smile had gone now, his deep, liquid voice low, and despite the full restaurant, despite the background noise of their fellow diners, it was as if they were the only two in the room.

His black eyes were working her face, appraising her, and she could almost imagine him walking towards her across the courtroom, circling her slowly, choosing the best method of attack. Fear did the strangest thing to Matilda, her lips twitching into a nervous smile as he again asked his question. 'You swear to answer me honestly.'

'I'm not on trial.' Matilda gave a tiny nervous laugh, but he remained unmoved.

'If we're going to play, we play by the rules.'

'Fine.' Matilda nodded. 'But I really think you're—'

'We've all got secrets,' Dante broke in softly. 'There's a dark side to every single one of us, and splash it on a headline, layer it with innuendo and suddenly we're all as guilty as hell. Take your ex—'

'Edward's got nothing to do—'

'Location, location, location.' He flashed a malevolent smile as Matilda's hand tightened convulsively around her glass. 'Just one more business dinner, just one more client to impress. Just one more garden to renovate and then, maybe then you'll get his attention. Maybe one day—'

'I don't need this,' Matilda said through gritted teeth. 'I've no idea what you're trying to get at, but can you please leave Edward out of this?'

'Still too raw?' He leant back in his chair, merciless eyes awaiting her response.

'No,' Matilda said tersely, leaning back into her own chair, *forcing* her tense shoulders to lower, *forcing* a smile onto her face. 'Absolutely not. Edward and I finished a couple of months ago. I'm completely over it.'

'Who ended it?'

'I did,' Matilda answered, but with renewed confidence now. She *had* been the one who had ended it, and that surely would thwart him, would rule out his image of a broken-hearted female who would go to any lengths to avoid confrontation.

'Why?' Dante asked bluntly, but Matilda gave a firm shake of her head.

'I'm not prepared to answer that,' she retorted coolly. 'I had my reasons. And in case you're wondering, no, there wasn't anyone else involved.' Confident she'd ended this line of questioning, sure he would try another tack, Matilda felt the fluttering butterflies in her stomach still a touch and her breathing slow down as she awaited his next question, determined to answer him with cool ease.

'Did you ever wish him dead?'

'What?' Appalled, she confronted him with her eyes—stunned that he would even ask such a thing. 'Of course not.'

'Are you honestly stating that you never once said that you wished that he was dead?'

'You're either mad…' Matilda let out an incredulous laugh '…or way too used to dealing with mad people! *Of course* I never said that I wished that he…' Her voice faltered for just a fraction of second, a flash of forgotten conversation pinging into consciousness, and like a cobra he struck.

'I'm calling your friend as a witness next—and I can assure you that her version of that night is completely different to yours…'

'What night?' Matilda scorned.

'*That* night,' Dante answered with absolute conviction, and Matilda felt her throat tighten as he spoke on. 'In fact, your friend clearly recalls a conversation where you expressed a strong wish that Edward was dead.' Dante's words were so measured, so assured, so absolutely spot on that for a tiny second she almost believed him. For a flash of time she almost expected to look over her shoulder and see Judy sitting at the other table, as if she had stumbled into some macabre reality TV show, where all her secrets, all her failings were about to be exposed.

Stop it, Matilda scolded herself, reining in her overreaction. Dante knew nothing about her. He was a skilled interrogator, that was all, used to finding people's Achilles' heels, and she wasn't going to let him. She damn well wasn't going to give him the satisfaction of breaking her.

'I still don't know what night you're talking about!'

'Then let me refresh your memory. I'm referring to the night you said that you wished Edward was dead.' And he didn't even make it sound like an assumption, his features so immovable it was as if he'd surely been in the room that night, as if he'd actually witnessed her raw tears, had heard every word she'd sobbed that night, as if somehow he was privy to her soul. 'And you did say that, didn't you, Matilda?'

To deny it would be an outright lie. Suddenly she wasn't sitting in a restaurant any more. Instead, she was back to where it had all ended two months ago, could feel the brutal slap of Edward's words as surely as if she were hearing them for the first time.

'Maybe if you weren't so damn frigid, I wouldn't have to look at other women to get my kicks.'

He'd taunted her, humiliated her, shamed her for her lack of sexual prowess, demeaned her with words so vicious, so brutal that by the time she'd run from his house, by the time she'd arrived at Judy's home, she'd believed each and every word. Believed that their relationship had been in trouble because of her failings, believed that if only she'd been prettier, sexier, funnier, he wouldn't have had to flirt so much, wouldn't have needed to humiliate her quite so badly. And somehow Dante knew it, too.

'You did say it, didn't you?' It was Dante's voice dragging her out of her own private hell.

'I just said it,' Matilda breathed, she could feel the blood draining out of her face. 'It was just one of those stupid things you say when you're angry.'

'And you were very angry, weren't you?'

'No,' Matilda refuted. 'I was upset and annoyed but angry is probably overstretching things.'

He swirled his wine around in the glass and Matilda's eyes darted towards it, watching the pale fluid whirl around the bottom, grateful for the distraction, grateful for something to focus on other than those dark, piercing eyes.

'So you were only upset and annoyed, yet you admit you wished him dead!'

'OK,' Matilda snapped, her head spinning as the barrage continued. 'I was angry, furious, in fact. So would anyone have been if they'd been told…' She choked her words down, refusing to drag up that shame and certainly not prepared to reveal it to Dante. Dragging in air, she halted her tirade, tried to remember to think before she spoke, to regain some of the control she'd so easily lost. 'Yes, I said that I wished he was dead, but there's a big difference between saying something and actually seeing it through.' She felt dizzy, almost sick with the emotions he'd so easily conjured up, like some wicked magician pulling out her past, her secrets, clandestine feelings exposed, and she didn't want it to continue, didn't want to partake in this a moment longer.

'Can we stop this now?' Her voice was high and slightly breathless, a trickle of moisture running between her breasts as she eyed this savage man, wondering how the hell he knew, how he had known so readily what buttons to push to reduce her to this.

'Any time you like.' Dante smiled, his voice so soft it was almost a caress, but it did nothing to soothe her. 'After all, it's just a game!'

The dessert was divine, the sweet sugary mousse contrasting with the sharp raspberry sauce, but Matilda was too shaken to really enjoy it, her long dessert spoon unusually lethargic as she attempted just to get through it.

'Is your dessert OK?'

'It's fine,' Matilda said, then gave in, putting her spoon down. 'Actually, I'm really not that hungry. I think I'll go home now…'

'I'm sorry if I destroyed your appetite.'

God, he had a nerve!

'No, you're not.' Matilda looked across the table at him and said it again. 'No, Dante, you're not. In fact I think that was exactly what you set out to do.' Reaching for her bag, Matilda stood up and picked up the roll of plans.

'I'll be at your house on Sunday afternoon. I'll look at the plans tomorrow but until I see the garden I really won't know what I'm going to do.'

'We've all said it.' Dante's smile bordered on the compassionate as she stood up to leave, and he didn't bother to elaborate—they both knew what he was referring to. 'And as you pointed out, there's a big difference between saying it and following it through. I was just proving a point.'

'Consider it proven,' Matilda replied with a very tight smile. 'Goodnight, Dante.'

Of course it took if not for ever then a good couple of minutes for the waiter to locate her jacket, giving Dante plenty of time to catch up with her. Rather than talk to him, she took a small after-dinner mint from the bowl on the desk, concentrating on unwrapping the thin gold foil as she prayed for the waiter to hurry up, popping the bitter chocolate into her mouth and biting into the sweet peppermint centre, then flushing as she sensed Dante watching her.

She'd said she wasn't hungry just two minutes ago— well, just because he was so damned controlled, it didn't mean that she had to be. What would a calculating man like Dante know about want rather than need? The man was utterly devoid of emotion, Matilda decided angrily. He probably peeled open his chest and pulled out his batteries at night, put them on charge ready to attack his next victim. Consoling herself that she could make a quick escape while he settled the bill, almost defiantly she took another chocolate, pathetically grateful when the waiter appeared with her jacket and helped her into it. She stepped outside into the night and closed her eyes as the cool night air hit her flaming cheeks.

'How far do you have to go?'

She heard Dante's footsteps as he came along behind her, recognised his heavily accented voice as he uttered the first syllable, his scent hitting her before he drew her aside, yet she'd known he was close long before, almost sensed his approach before he'd made himself known.

'How did you…?' She didn't finish her question, didn't want to be drawn into another conversation with him. She just marched swiftly on, her stilettos making a tinny sound as she clipped along the concrete pavement.

'I eat regularly there. They send my account out once a month or so and my secretary deals with it.'

The one who'd dared to allow herself to get pregnant, Matilda wanted to point out, but chose not to, clutching the plans tighter under her arm and walking swiftly on.

'Would you like a lift home?'

'I have an apartment over the bridge.' Matilda pointed to the a high-rise block on the other side of the river. 'It's just a five-minute walk.'

'Then I'll join you,' Dante said. 'You shouldn't be walking alone across the bridge at this time of night.'

'Really,' Matilda flustered, 'there's absolutely no need—it's just a hop and a skip.'

'I'd rather *walk* if you don't mind,' Dante said, his face completely deadpan, but his dry humour didn't even raise a smile from Matilda. Frankly, she'd rather take the chance of walking across the bridge alone than with the evil troll beside her.

'I have an apartment near here also,' Dante said, nodding backwards from whence they'd come, but despite the proximity to hers, Matilda was quite sure any city apartment Dante owned wouldn't compare to her second-floor shoebox!

'I didn't somehow envisage you as having an apartment,' Dante mused, and Matilda blinked, surprised he *envisaged* her at all. 'I thought, given your work you would have a home with a garden.'

'That's the plan, actually,' Matilda admitted. 'I've just put it up for sale. I never really liked it.'

'So why did you buy it?'

'It was too good an opportunity to miss. And location-wise, for work it's brilliant.' She gave a low groan at the sound of her own voice. 'Can you tell I spent the last couple of years dating a real estate agent?' Matilda asked, glancing over to him and surprised to see that he was actually smiling.

'At least you didn't mention the stunning views and the abundance of natural light!'

'Only because I'm on the second floor,' Matilda quipped, amazed after the tension of only a few moments ago to find herself actually smiling back. 'I guess the drive from Mount Eliza to the city each day would be a bit much,' Matilda ventured, but again she got things wrong.

'I don't generally drive to work, I use a helicopter.'

'Of course you do,' Matilda sighed, rolling her eyes.

'It is not my helicopter.' She could hear the teasing note in his voice. 'More like a taxi service. I would rather spend that hour or two at home than in the car. When we bought the place it was meant more as weekender, or retreat, but since the accident I have tried not to move Alex too much. It is better, I think that she is near the beach with lots of space rather than the city. A luxury high rise apartment isn't exactly stimulating for a small child.'

Why did he always make her feel small?

'I use the apartment a lot, though. I tend to stay there if I am involved in a difficult trial.'

'I guess it would be quieter.'

'A bit,' Dante admitted. 'I tend to get very absorbed in my cases. By the time they go to trial there is not much space left for anything else. But it is not just for that reason.' They were walking quickly, too quickly for Matilda, who almost had to run to keep up with him, but she certainly wasn't going to ask him to slow down. The sooner they got to her apartment block the sooner she could breathe again. 'The press can be merciless at times. I prefer to keep it away from my family.'

They were safely over the bridge now, walking along the dark embankment on the other side of the river.

'This is me,' Matilda said as they neared her apartment block, and she rummaged in her bag for her keys. 'I'll be fine now.'

'I'm sure that you would be,' Dante said, 'but you are my dinner guest and for that reason I will see you safely home.'

Why did he have to display manners now? Matilda wondered. He'd been nothing but rude since they'd met—it was a bit late for chivalry. But she was too drained to argue, just gave a resigned shrug, let herself into the entrance hall and headed for the stairwell, glad that she lived on the second floor and therefore wouldn't have to squeeze into a lift with him again.

'Home!' Matilda said with false brightness.

'Do you always take the stairs?'

'Always,' Matilda lied. 'It's good exercise.' They were at her front door now. 'Thank you for this evening. It's been, er…pleasant.'

'Really?' Dante raised a quizzical eyebrow. 'I'm not sure that I believe you.'

'I was actually attempting to be polite,' Matilda responded, 'as you were by seeing me to my door.' She was standing there, staring at him, willing him to just go, reluctant somehow to turn her back on him, not scared exactly, but on heightened alert as still he just stood there. Surely he didn't expect her to ask him in for coffee?

Surely!

How the hell was she going to spend a fortnight in

his company when one evening left her a gibbering wreck? She *had* to get a grip, had to bring things back to a safer footing, had to let him know that it was strictly business, pretend that he didn't intimidate her, pretend that he didn't move her so.

'Thank you for bringing the plans, Dante. I'm looking forward to working on your garden.' She offered her hand. Direct, businesslike, Matilda decided, that was how she'd be—a snappy end to a business dinner. But as his hand took hers, instantly she regretted it.

It was only the second time they had made physical contact. As his hand tightened around hers she was brutally reminded of that fact, despite the hours that had passed, despite a dinner shared and the emotions he had evoked, it was only the second time they had touched. And the result was as explosive as the first time, and many times more lethal. She could feel the heat of his flesh searing into hers, as his large hand coiled around hers, the pad of his index finger resting on her slender wrist, her radial pulse hammering against it. And this time the feel of his gold wedding band did nothing to soothe her, just reminded her of the depths of him, the pain that must surely exist behind those indecipherable eyes. Never had she found a person so difficult to read, never had she revealed so much of herself to someone and found out so very little in return.

But she wanted to know more.

'You interest me, Matilda.' It was such a curious thing to say, such a hazy, ambiguous statement, and her eyes involuntarily jerked to his like a reflex action, held by his gaze, stunned, startled, yet curiously reluctant to move, a heightened sexual awareness permeating her.

'I thought perhaps I bored you.'

'Oh, no.' Slowly he shook his head and she started back, mesmerised, his sensuous but brutal features utterly captivating. 'Why would you think such a thing?'

'I just…' Matilda's voice trailed off. She didn't know what to say because she didn't know the answer, didn't know if it was her destroyed self-confidence that made her vulnerable or the man who was staring at her now, the man who was pinning her to the wall with his eyes.

'He really hurt you, didn't he?' It was as if he were staring into her very soul, not asking her but telling her how she felt. 'He ground you down and down until you didn't even know who you were any more, didn't even know what it was that you wanted.'

How did he know? How could he read her so easily—was she that predictable? Was her pain, her self-doubt so visible? But Dante hadn't finished with his insights, hadn't finished peeling away the layers, exposing her raw, bruised core, and she wanted again to halt him, wanted to stop him from going further— wanted that mouth that was just inches from hers be silent, to kiss her…

'And then, when he'd taken every last drop from you, he tossed you aside…'

She shook her head in denial, relieved that he'd got one thing wrong. 'I was the one who ended it,' Matilda reminded him, but it didn't sway him for a second.

'You just got there first.' Dante delivered his knockout blow. 'It was already over.'

He was right, of course, it had been over. She could still feel the bleak loneliness that had filled her that night and for many nights before the final one. The indifference had been so much more painful that the rows that had preceded it. She could still feel the raw shame of Edward's intimate rejections.

'I'm fine without him.'

'Better than fine,' Dante said softly, and she held her breath as that cruel, sensual mouth moved in towards hers. She still didn't know what he was thinking. Lust rippled between them, yet his expression was completely unreadable. The same quiver of excitement that had gripped her in the restaurant shivered through her now, but with dangerous sexual undertones, and it was inevitable they would kiss. Matilda acknowledged it then. The foreplay she had so vehemently denied was taking place had started hours ago, long, long before they'd even reached the garden.

He gave her time to move away, ample time to halt things, to stop this now, and she should have.

Normally she would have.

Her mind flitted briefly to her recent attempts at dating where she'd dreaded this moment, had avoided it or gone along with a kiss for the sad sake of it, to prove to herself that she was desirable perhaps.

But there was no question here of merely going along with this kiss for the sake of it—logic, common sense, self-preservation told her that to end *this* night with a kiss was a foolish move, that for the sake of her sanity she should surely halt this now. But her body told her otherwise, every nerve prickling to delicious attention, drawn like a magnet to his beauty, anticipating the taste of him, the feel of him in a heady rush of need, of want.

His mouth brushed her cheek, sweeping along her cheekbone till she could feel his breath warm on the shell of her ear then moving back, back to her waiting lips, slowly, deliberately until only a whisper separated them, till his mouth was so close to hers that she was giddy with expectation, filled with want—deep, burning want that she'd never yet experienced, a want that suffused her, a want she had never, even in the most intimate moments, experienced, and he hadn't even kissed her. Her breath was coming in short, unyielding gasps, his chest so close to hers that if she breathed any deeper their bodies would touch. She was torn between want and dread, her body longing to arch towards his, her nipples stretching like buds to the sun, his hand still on the wall behind her head, and all she wanted was his touch.

As if in answer, his mouth found hers, the weight of his body pushing her down, his lips obliterating thought, reason, question, his masterful touch the only thought she could process, his tongue, stroking hers so deeply so intimately it was as if he were touching her deep inside, his skin dragging hers as his mouth moved against her, the sweet, decadent taste of him, the heady masculine scent of him stroking her awake from deep hibernation, awareness fizzing in where there had been none.

His power overwhelmed her, the strength of his arms around her slender body, the hard weight of his thighs as he pinned her to the wall and a vague peripheral awareness of a warm hand creeping along the length of her spinal column then sliding around her rib cage as his mouth worked ever on. A low needy sigh built as it slid around, his palm capturing the weight of her breast, the

warmth of his skin through the sheer fabric of her dress
had her curling into him, needy, wanton, desperate,
swelling at his touch, her breasts engorging, shamefully
reciprocating as the pad of his thumb teased her jutting
nipple. So many sensations, so many responses, his
tongue capturing hers in his lips, sucking on the swollen
tip, his body pinning her in delicious confinement, his
masculinity capturing her, overwhelming her. Yet she
was hardly an unwilling participant—fingers coiling in
his jet hair, pulling his face to hers as her body pressed
against him, his touch unleashing her passion, her desire,
flaming it to dangerous heat, a heat so intense there was
no escape, and neither did she want one. His kiss was
everything a kiss should be, everything she'd missed.

Till now.

And just as she dived into complete oblivion, just as
she would have given anything, anything for this
moment to continue, for him to douse the fire within her,
he wrenched his head away, an expression she couldn't
read in his eyes as he looked coolly down at her.

'I should go.'

Words failing her, Matilda couldn't even nod, embarrassment creeping in now. He could have taken her there
and then—with one crook of his manicured finger she
would have led him inside, would have made love to him,
would have let him make love to her. What was it with
this man? Emotionally he troubled her, terrified her even,
yet still she was drawn to him, physically couldn't resist
him. She had never felt such compulsion, a macabre ad-
diction almost, and she hadn't even know him a day.

'I will see you on Sunday.' His voice was completely

normal and his hands were still on her trembling body. She stared back at him, unable to fathom that he could appear so unmoved, that he was still standing after what they'd just shared. Blindly she nodded, her hair tumbling down around her face, eyes frowning as Dante reached into his suit pocket and pulled out a handful of chocolate mints, the same ones she had surreptitiously taken at the restaurant.

'I took these at the restaurant for you…' Taking her hand, he filled it with the sweet chocolate delicacies. She could feel them soft and melting through the foil as he closed her fingers around them. 'I know you wanted to do the same!'

An incredulous smile broke onto her lips at the gesture, a tiny glimmer that maybe things were OK, that the attraction really was mutual, that Dante didn't think any less of her because of what had just taken place. 'You stole them?' Matilda gave a tiny half-laugh, recalling their earlier conversation.

'Oh, no.' He shook his head and doused any fledgling hope with one cruel sentence, cheapened and humiliated her with his strange euphemism. 'Why would I steal them when, after all, they were there for the taking?'

CHAPTER FOUR

WHAT she had been expecting, Matilda wasn't sure—
an austere, formal residence, surrounded by an overgrown wilderness, or a barren landscape perhaps—but
with directions on the passenger seat beside her she'd
found the exclusive street fairly easily and had caught
her breath as she'd turned into it, The heavenly view of
Port Phillip Bay stretched out for ever before her.
Chewing on her lip as she drove, the sight of the opulent,
vast houses of the truly rich forced her to slow down as
she marvelled at the architecture and stunning gardens,
tempted to whip out her faithful notepad and jot down
some notes and deciding that soon she would do just
that. The thought of long evenings with nothing to do
but avoid Dante was made suddenly easier. She could
walk along the beach with her pad, even wander down
to one of the many cafés she had passed as she'd driven
through the village—there was no need to be alone with
him, no need at all.

Unless she wanted to be.

Pulling into the kerb, Matilda raked a hand through
her hair, tempted, even at the eleventh hour, to execute

a hasty U-turn and head for the safety of home. Since she'd awoken on Saturday after a restless sleep, she'd been in a state of high anxiety, especially when she'd opened the newspaper and read with renewed interest about the sensational trial that was about to hit the Melbourne courts and realising that it wasn't just her that was captivated by Dante Costello. Apart from the salacious details of the upcoming trial, a whole article had been devoted solely to Dante, and the theatre that this apparently brilliant man created, from his scathing tongue and maverick ways in the courtroom to the chameleon existence he'd had since the premature death of his beloved wife, his abrupt departure from the social scene, his almost reclusive existence, occasionally fractured by the transient presence of a beautiful woman— anodynes, Matilda had guessed, that offered a temporary relief. And though it had hurt like hell to read it, Matilda had devoured it, gleaning little, understanding less. The face that had stared back at her from the newspaper pages had been as distant and as unapproachable as the man she had first met and nothing, *nothing* like the Dante who had held her in his arms, who had kissed her to within an inch of her life, who had so easily awoken the woman within—the real Dante she was sure she'd glimpsed.

Matilda had known that the sensible thing to do would be to ring Hugh and tell him she couldn't do the work after all—that something else had come up. Hell, she had even dialled his number a few times, but at the last minute had always hung up, torn between want and loathing, outrage and desire, telling herself that it wouldn't be fair to let Hugh down, and sometimes almost managing to believe it. As honourable as it sounded, loyalty to Hugh had nothing to do with her being there today. Dante totally captivated her—since the second she'd laid eyes on him he was *all* she thought about.

All she thought about, replaying their conversations over and over, jolting each and every time she recalled some of his sharper statements, wondering how the hell he managed to get away with it, how she hadn't slapped his arrogant cheek. And yet somehow there had been a softer side and it was that that intrigued her. Despite his brutality she'd glimpsed something else—tiny flickers of beauty, like flowers in a desert—his dry humour, the stunning effect of his occasional smile on her, the undeniable tenderness reserved exclusively for his daughter. And, yes, Matilda acknowledged that the raw, simmering passion that had been in his kiss had left her hungry for more,

'Careful.' Matilda said the word out loud, repeated it over and over in her mind as she slipped the car into first gear and slowly pulled out into the street, driving a couple of kilometres further with her heart in her mouth as she braced herself to face him again, her hand shaking slightly as she turned into his driveway and pressed the intercom, watching unblinking as huge metal gates slid open and she glimpsed for the first time Dante's stunning home.

The drive was as uncompromising and as rigid as its owner, lined with cypress trees drawing the eye along its vast, straight length to the huge, Mediterranean-looking residence—vast white rendered walls that made the sky look bluer somehow, massive floor-to-ceiling windows that would drench the home in light and let in every inch of the stunning view. She inched her way along, momentarily forgetting her nerves, instead absorbing the beauty. The harsh lines of the house were softened at the entrance by climbers—wisteria, acres of it, ambled across the front of the property, heavy lilac flowers hanging like bunches of grapes, intermingled with jasmine, its creamy white petals like dotted stars, the more delicate foliage competing with the harsh wooden branches of the wisteria. The effect, quite simply, was divine.

'Welcome!' Hugh pulled open the car door for her and Matilda stepped out onto the white paved driveway, pathetically grateful to see him—not quite ready to face Dante alone. 'Matilda, this is my wife Katrina.' He introduced a tall, elegant woman who stepped forward and shook her hand, her greeting the antithesis of Hugh's warm one. Cool blue eyes blatantly stared Matilda up and down, taking in the pale blue cotton shift dress and casual sandals she was wearing and clearly not liking what she saw. 'You're nothing like I was expecting. I expected…' she gave a shrill laugh… 'I don't know. You don't look like a gardener!'

'She's a designer, Katrina,' Hugh said with a slight edge.

'I'm very hands-on, though,' Matilda said. 'I like to see the work through from beginning to end.'

'Marvellous,' Katrina smiled, but somehow her face remained cold. 'Come—let me introduce you to Dante…'

Matilda was about to say that she'd already met

him, but decided against it, as clearly both Hugh and Dante had omitted to mention the dinner to Katrina. She wasn't sure what to make of Katrina. She was stunning-looking, her posture was straight, her long hair, though dashed with grey, was still an amazing shade of strawberry blonde, and though she had to be around fifty, there was barely a line on her smooth face. But there was a frostiness about her that unsettled Matilda.

The interior of the house was just as impressive as the exterior. Hugh held open the front door then headed off to Matilda's car to retrieve her bags and the two women stepped inside and walked along the jarrah-floored hallways, Matilda's sandals echoing on the solid wood as she took in the soft white sofas and dark wooden furnishings, huge mirrors opening up the already vast space, reflecting the ocean at every turn so that wherever you looked the waves seemed to beckon. Or Jasmine smiled down at you! An inordinate number of photos of Dante's late wife adorned the walls, her gorgeous face captured from every angle, and Matilda felt a quiet discomfort as she gazed around, her cheeks flaming as she recalled the stinging kiss of Dante.

'My daughter.' Katrina's eyes followed Matilda's and they paused for a moment as they admired her tragic beauty. 'I had this photo blown up and framed just last week—it's good for Alex to be able to see her and I know it gives Dante a lot of comfort.'

'It must…' Matilda stumbled. 'She really was very beautiful.'

'And clever,' Katrina added. 'She had it all, brains

and beauty. She was amazing, a wonderful mother and wife. None of us will ever get over her loss.'

'I can't even begin to imagine…' Despite the cool breeze from the air-conditioner, despite the high ceilings and vastness of the place, Matilda felt incredibly hot and uncomfortable. Despite her earlier misgivings, she was very keen to meet Dante now—even his savage personality was preferable to the discomfort she felt with Katrina.

'Dante especially,' Katrina continued, and Matilda was positive, despite her soft words and pensive smile, that there was a warning note to her voice, an icy message emanating from her cool blue eyes. 'I've never seen a man so broken with grief. He just adored her, *adored* her,' Katrina reiterated. 'Do you know, the day she died he sent flowers to her office. It was a Saturday but she had to pop into work and get some files. She took Alex with her—that was the sort of woman she was. Anyway, Dante must have rung every florist in Melbourne. He wanted to send her some jasmine, her namesake, but it was winter, of course, so it was impossible to find, but Dante being Dante he managed to organise it—he'd have moved heaven and earth for her.'

It was actually a relief to get into the kitchen. After Katrina's onslaught it was actually a relief to confront the man she'd been so nervous of meeting again. But as she stepped inside it was as if she was seeing him for the very first time. The man she remembered bore little witness to the one she saw now. Everything about him seemed less formal. Of course, she hadn't expected him to greet her in a suit—it was Sunday after all—but somehow she'd never envisaged him in jeans and a T-shirt, or, if she had, it would have been in dark, starched denim and a crisp white designer label T-shirt, not the faded, scruffy jeans that encased him, not the untucked, unironed white T-shirt that he was wearing. And she certainly hadn't pictured him at a massive wooden table, kneading bread, with his daughter, Alex's eyes staring ahead as she rhythmically worked the dough.

'Dante, Alexandra,' Katrina called. 'Matilda has arrived.'

Only one pair of eyes looked up. Alexandra carried on kneading the dough and any thought of witnessing Dante's softer side was instantly quashed as his black eyes briefly met hers.

'Good afternoon.'

His greeting was also his dismissal.

His attention turning immediately back to his daughter, picking up a large shaker and sprinkling the dough with more flour as the little girl worked on.

'Good afternoon.' Matilda forced a smile to no one in particular. 'You're making bread…'

'No.' Dante stood up, dusted his floured hands on his jeans 'We are kneading dough and playing with flour.'

'Oh!'

'We've been kneading dough and playing with flour since lunchtime, actually!'

Another 'oh' was on the tip of her tongue, but Matilda held it back, grateful when Katrina took over this most awkward of conversations.

'It's one of Alex's pastimes,' Katrina explained as

Hugh came back in. 'She was upset after lunch—you know what children can be like.' Dante gave a tight smile as Katrina dismissed the slightly weary note to his voice. Something told Matilda that whatever had eventuated had been rather more than the usual childhood tantrum. 'Hugh, why don't you go and take Matilda around the garden?' Katrina said. 'It seems a shame to break things up when Dante and Alex are having such fun.'

'Hugh's supposed to be resting,' Dante pointed out. '*I'll* take Matilda around.'

'Fine,' Katrina said, though clearly it was anything but! 'Then I'll go and check that everything's in order in the summerhouse for Matilda.'

'The summerhouse?' Dante frowned. 'I had the guest room made up for her. Janet prepared it this morning.'

'Well, it won't kill Janet to prepare the summerhouse! She's the housekeeper,' Katrina explained to a completely bemused Matilda. 'I can help her set it up. It will be far nicer for Matilda. She can have some privacy and it might unsettle Alex, having a stranger in the house—no offence meant, Matilda.'

'None taken.' Matilda thought her face might crack with the effort of smiling. 'It really doesn't matter a scrap where I stay. I'm going to be working long hours, I just need somewhere to sleep and eat…'

'There's a lovely little kitchenette in the summerhouse. I'll have some bacon and eggs and bread put in, that type of thing—you'll be very comfortable.'

'It's your fault.' Dante broke the appalling silence as they stepped outside.

'What is?' Matilda blinked.

'That you've been banished.' He gave her a glimmer of a dry smile. 'You're too good-looking for Katrina.'

'Oh!' A tiny nervous giggle escaped her lips, embarrassed by what he had said but relieved all the same that he had acknowledged the problem. 'I don't think she likes me very much.'

'She'd have been hoping for a ruddy-faced, gum-chewing, crop-haired gardener. I have the ugliest staff in the world—all hand-picked by Katrina.' Startled by his coarseness, Matilda actually laughed as they walked, amazed to find herself relaxing a touch in his presence.

'Yesterday's newspapers can't have helped matters much,' she ventured, referring to the string of women he'd dated since his wife's death, but Dante just shrugged.

'Ships that pass in the night even Katrina can live with.'

The callousness of his words had Matilda literally stopping in her tracks for a moment, waiting for him to soften it with a smile, to tell her he was joking, but Dante strode on, forcing Matilda to catch him up, and try to continue the conversation. 'Do your in-laws live here with you?'

'God, no.' Dante shuddered. 'They live a few kilometres away. But we're interviewing for a new nanny at the moment—preferably one over sixty with a wooden leg if Katrina has her way. That's why she's around so much. Like it or not at the moment I do need her help with Alex, but if I decide to stay here in Australia…' He stopped talking then, just simply stopped in mid-sentence with no apology or explanation, clearly deciding he had said enough. Silence descended again as they walked on the manicured lawn past a massive pool, surrounded by a clear Perspex wall. Matilda gazed at the pool longingly.

'Use it any time,' Dante offered.

'Thanks,' Matilda replied, knowing full well she wouldn't. The thought of undressing, of wearing nothing more than a bikini around Dante not exactly soothing.

'This is the garden,' Dante said as they came to a gate. 'It's in a real mess, very neglected, overgrown with blackberries and bracken, I've been meaning to get it cleared, but my gardener is getting old. It takes all his time just to keep up with the regular work, let alone this. Oh, and one other thing…' His hand paused on the gate. 'The bill is to come to me.'

'Hugh employed me,' Matilda pointed out.

'Hugh does not need to pay for my renovations—you will send the bill to me, Matilda.'

But she didn't want to send the bill to him—and it had nothing to do with money. Financially it made not a scrap of difference to Matilda who picked up the bill. Instead, it was the disturbing thought of being answerable somehow to Dante, of him employing her, that made Matilda strangely nervous.

'Do you need an advance?'

'An advance?' Instantly, she regretted her words. Her mind had been utterly elsewhere and now she sounded stupid.

'An advance of money,' Dante not too patiently explained. 'To pay the subcontractors. I don't know what arrangement you had with Hugh—'

'*Have* with Hugh,' Matilda corrected, watching as Dante's face darkened. Clearly he was not used to being defied, but even though an advance would be wonderful now, even though she had a hundred and one people that would need to be paid, and very soon, she damn well wasn't going to give in to him, absolutely refused to let him dictate his terms to her. 'My business is with Hugh. If you want to settle up with him, that's your choice.'

Surprisingly he didn't argue, but as he pushed open the gate she could tell he was far from pleased, but, refusing to back down, refusing to even look at him, she stepped into the garden and as she did all thoughts of money and who was the boss faded in an instant. Despite Dante's gloomy predictions, all she could see was beauty—the sleeping princess that lay beneath the overgrown bracken and thorns.

Dante's manicured gardens were wonderful, but, for Matilda, nothing could beat the raw natural beauty of a neglected garden, a blank canvas for her to work on. It was about the size of a suburban block of land, the centrepiece a massive willow, more than a hundred years in the making, one lifetime simply not enough to produce its full majesty. But that was part of the beauty of her work. A new garden was a mere a sketch on the canvas—the colour, the depth was added over the years, seeds sown that would flourish later, shrubs, trees that would develop, blossom and grow long, long after the cheque had been paid and her tools cleared away.

'Vistas.' It was the first thing that came to mind and she said it out loud, registering his frown. 'Lots of walkways all coming from the willow, lined with hedges and each one leading to a different view, a special area for Alex…'

'You can do something with it?'

She didn't answer, just gave a distracted nod as she pictured the bosky paths, a water feature at the end of one, a sand pit at the end of the other, and…

'A castle,' Matilda breathed. 'An enchanted castle, like a fairy-tale. I know someone who makes the most beautiful cubby houses…' Her voice trailed off as she stared down at the ground, her sandals scuffing the earth. 'We'll use turf for now, but I'll plant lots of different things so that each path will be different—clover for one, daisies for another, buttercups…'

'Will you be able to do it in the time-frame?'

Matilda nodded. 'Less perhaps. I'll know more tomorrow once it's cleared. I've got some people coming at six. There'll be a lot of noise, but only tomorrow…'

'That's fine. Katrina has already said she will take Alex out or to her place during the day. You'll have the place to yourself…' He paused and Matilda wondered if he was going to raise the money issue again, but instead it was a rather more difficult subject he brought up. 'I'm sorry she made you feel uncomfortable.'

'She didn't,' Matilda attempted, then gave in as he raised a questioning eyebrow. 'OK, she did make me feel a bit uncomfortable, but it's fine.'

'I'll take you and show you the summerhouse. But you don't have to cook for yourself, you're very welcome to come over for—'

'I'll be fine,' Matilda interrupted. 'In fact, it's probably better that I stay there…' Blowing her fringe skyward, Matilda attempted the impossible but, ever direct, Dante beat her to it.

'After what happened on Friday?' He checked and despite a deep blush Matilda gave a wry smile.

'I don't think Katrina would approve somehow if she knew. She doesn't even know that we had dinner, let alone…'

'It's none of Katrina's business,' Dante pointed out, but Matilda shook her head.

'Oh, but she thinks it is.'

'Matilda.' His black eyes were boring into her, and she could only admire his boldness that he could actually look at her, unlike she, herself, who gave in after once glance, choosing instead to stare at her toes as he spoke. 'I will tell you what I told Katrina. I have no interest in a relationship—any relationship. For now I grieve for what I have lost: a wife and the happiness of my daughter.' Still she looked down, swallowing down the questions that were on the tip of her tongue. But either he could read her mind or he had used this speech many times before, because he answered each and every one of them with painful, brutal honesty, his silken, thick accent doing nothing to sweeten the bitterness of the message.

'I like women—I like beautiful women,' he drawled, wrapping the knife that stabbed her in velvet as he plunged it in. 'And as you would have seen in the paper yesterday, sometimes I keep their company, but there is always concurrence, always there is an understanding that it can go nowhere. If I misled you on Friday, I apologise.'

'You didn't mislead me.' Matilda croaked the words out then instantly regretted them. In that split second she understood what Dante was offering her, what this emotionally abstinent man was telling her—that she could have him for a short while, could share his bed, but not his heart. And all Matilda knew was that she couldn't do it, couldn't share his bed knowing she must walk away, that deadening his pain would only exacerbate hers. His hand reached out towards her, his fingers cupping her chin, lifting her face to his. Yet she still refused to look at him, knew that if her eyes met his then she'd be lost.

'You didn't mislead me, Dante, because it was just a kiss.' Somehow she kept her voice even; somehow she managed to keep her cheeks from flaming as she lied through her teeth. 'A kiss to end the evening. I certainly had no intention of taking things further, either then or now.' She knew she hadn't convinced him and from the slight narrowing of his eyes knew that he didn't believe her. Taking a breath, she elaborated, determined to set the tone, and the boundaries in order to survive the next couple of weeks. She didn't want to be one of Dante's ships that passed in the night. 'Since Edward and I broke up, I've been on a few dates, had a few kisses, but…' Matilda gave a nervous shrug. 'You know the saying: you have to kiss a lot of frogs…' From his slightly startled look clearly he didn't know it. 'One kiss was enough for me, Dante.'

'I see.' He gave a tight smile. 'I think.'

'It won't be happening again,' Matilda affirmed, hoping that if she said it enough she might even believe it herself.

'I just wanted to clear things up.'

'Good.' Matilda forced a bright smile, relieved this torture was almost over. 'I'm glad that you did.'

'And I'm sorry that you did not enjoy the kiss.' His words wiped the smile from her face, his eyes boring into her. She couldn't be sure, but Matilda was positive he was teasing her, that he knew she was lying and, of course, she was. It had been the most breathtaking kiss of her life, her whole body was burning now just at the mere memory, but it was imperative Dante didn't know. He'd made it clear he wasn't interested in anything more than the most casual of casual flings, and that was the last thing she needed now—especially with a man like Dante. There was nothing casual about him, nothing casual about the feelings he evoked, and if she played with this particular fire, Matilda knew she'd end up seriously burnt. 'Because I thought that—'

'Could you show me where I'm staying, please?' Matilda snapped, following Dante's lead and refusing to be drawn somewhere she didn't want to go. She turned abruptly to go, but in her haste to escape she forgot about the blackberries. Her leg caught on a branch, the thorn ripping into her bare calf, a yelp of pain escaping her lips.

'Careful.' Dante's reflexes were like lightning. He pulled back the branch and held her elbow as Matilda stepped back and instinctively inspected the damage, tears of pain and embarrassment filling her eyes at the vivid red gash.

'I'm fine,' she breathed.

'You're bleeding.'

'It's just a scratch. If you can just show me where I'm staying…' she said. She almost shouted it this time she so badly wanted out of there, wanted some privacy from his knowing eyes, but Dante was pulling out a neatly folded hanky and running it under the garden tap, before returning and dropping to his knees.

'Please.' Matilda was practically begging now, near to tears, not with pain but with embarrassment and want, the thought of him touching her exquisitely unbearable. But Dante wasn't listening. One hand cupped her calf, the other pressed the cool silk into her stinging cut, and it was as soothing as it was disturbing—the ultimate pleasure-pain principle as his hands tended her, calming and arousing. Matilda bit so hard on her lip she thought she might draw blood there, too, her whole body tense, standing rigid as he pressed the handkerchief harder, her stomach a knot of nervous anticipation as she felt his breath against her thigh.

'I'll just press for a minute and stop the bleeding, then I'll take you over to the summerhouse…' Strange that his voice was completely normal, that his body was completely relaxed, while hers was spinning in wild orbit, stirred with naked lust, shameful, inappropriate thoughts filling her mind as he tended her. She couldn't believe her own thought process as she stood there, gazing down. His fingers were pushed into her calf as the cool silk pressed on her warm skin, his breath on her leg as he spoke. And how she wanted to feel that delicious mouth again, but on her thigh this time, almost willing with her eyes for his fingers to creep higher, to quell the pulse that was leaping between her legs, to calm the heat with his cool, cool hand. 'I think there's a first-aid box…'

'I'll be OK.' She shivered the words out.

'Of course you will, it's just a cut, but…' His voice faded as he looked up at her, his eyes fixing on hers. And she stared back, trapped like a deer in the headlights, knowing he could feel it now, could see her treacherous arousal, could smell her excitement, *knew* that she had lied when she had said she didn't want him.

The silence fizzed between them as he continued to stare, and for that moment the choice was entirely his— reason, logic, had gone the second he'd touched her. If Dante pulled her down now, they both knew that she wouldn't even attempt to resist…

'Matilda…' His voice was thick with lust, his eyes blatantly desiring her. Thank God he spoke, thank God he broke the spell, gave her that tiny moment to stab at self-preservation and pull back her leg. Her face flaming she turned around, denied absolutely what was taking place, turning and heading for the gate, practically wrenching it open, just desperate for some space, some distance, a chance to think before her body betrayed her again.

There for the taking.

Those were the words he'd taunted her with on Friday night and those were the words that taunted her now as he led her over to the summerhouse and briefly showed her around.

As the door closed on Dante, not even looking at her surroundings, Matilda sank onto the bed and buried her face in her hands, cringing with shame, as sure as she could be that Dante had witnessed her arousal, had sensed her desire.

What was wrong with her? She wasn't even, according to Edward, supposed to like sex, yet here she was acting like some hormone-laden teenage girl with a king-sized crush, contemplating an affair with a man who wanted nothing more than her body.

And *how* she was contemplating! Despite her attempts at indifference, despite her brave words before, she wanted him. But unlike Dante, it wasn't just bed she wanted but the prelude to it and the postscript afterwards, the parts of him he wasn't prepared to give.

For the first time she took in her surroundings. The summerhouse was certainly comfortable—in fact, it was gorgeous. A cedar attic-shaped building, tucked away at the rear of the property, no doubt it had once been a rather impressive shed, but it had been lovingly refurbished, the attention to detail quite amazing. A small kitchenette as you entered, and to the left a small *en suite* with a shower, the rest of the floor space taken up by a large bed and a television and CDs. Janet, the rather prim housekeeper, came over with her bags and filled up the fridge with produce, explaining that the previous owners had used it as a bed and breakfast, but since the Costellos had owned it, for the most part it had remained empty.

'Mr Costello wanted to know if you'll be joining him for dinner,' Janet said, once she had stocked up the fridge with enough food to feed a small army. 'It's served at seven-thirty once young Alex is in bed, except for Tuesdays and Thursdays. I have my bible class on those nights…'

'No,' Matilda quickly answered, then softened her rather snappy response with a smile. 'I mean, tell him, no, thank you,' she added.

'I'll bring your dinner over to you,' Janet offered, but Matilda stood firm.

'There's really no need. I'll just have a sandwich or something, or go out to one of the cafés.'

'As you wish.' Janet shrugged as she headed out the door. 'But if you need anything, just ring through.'

Alone, Matilda changed into her working clothes— a pair of faded denim shorts that had seen better days and a flimsy T-shirt, topping the rather unflattering ensemble off with a pair of socks and her workboots. She poked her tongue out at her reflection in the mirror—at least Katrina would be pleased! Grateful for the diversion of the garden to take her mind off Dante, she turned on her mobile, winced at the rather full message bank, then promptly chose to ignore it, instead ringing the various people she would be needing, firming up a time with Declan to bring his bob-cat and confirming the large number of skips she had ordered to be delivered at Dante's in the morning. Then she headed off to the garden armed with a notebook and tape measure, ready to turn her vision into the plans that would become a reality. She lost herself for hours, as she always did when a project engrossed her, only downing tools and heading for the summerhouse when the last fingers of light had faded, hot, thirsty and exhausted, ready for a long, cool drink, followed by a long cool shower…

But not a cold one!

Yelping in alarm, Matilda fiddled with the taps, but to no avail, realising with a sinking heart that no amount of wishful thinking was going to change things: the hot-water system really wasn't working. Grabbing a towel,

Matilda wrapped it around her and sat shivering on the bed, trying and failing to decide what on earth to do. If she had been here for a couple of weeks to type up notes or fix some accounts then somehow she'd have struggled through, but even if her business cards screamed the words 'landscape designer,' at the end of the day gardening was a dirty job—filthy at times. And a fortnight of black nails and grit in her hair wasn't a prospect Matilda relished. Of course, the obvious thing to do would be to ring Janet and explain the situation but, then, there was nothing *obvious* about this situation—the absolute last place she wanted to be was crossing Dante's manicured lawn clutching her toiletry bag! Eyeing the kettle, Matilda rolled her eyes, the irony of her situation hitting home as she filled the tiny sink and swished a bar of soap around to make bubbles— here she was in a multi-million dollar home, and washing like a pauper!

CHAPTER FIVE

GOD, it was hot.

Matilda filled up her water bottle from the tap and surveyed the barren scene.

The morning had been crisp—par for the course in Melbourne. Used to the elements, she'd layered her clothing—gallons of sunscreen, followed by boots and shorts, a crop top, a T-shirt, a long-sleeved top, a jumper and a hat. Up at the crack of dawn, she'd greeted the workers and given her directions. Money wasn't the problem, time was, so a small army had been hired for the messy job of clearing the site. They all worked well, the skips filling quickly. As the day warmed up the jumper was the first to go, followed an hour or so later by her cotton top, and as each layer of clothing came off Matilda, so too did the garden start to emerge— until finally, long since down to her crop top, the late afternoon sun burning into her shoulders, Matilda surveyed her exhausting day's work. The subcontractors had finally gone, the skips noisily driven away, leaving the site bare and muddy apart from the gorgeous willow. At last she had her blank canvas!

Gulping on her water bottle, Matilda walked around the site, checking the fence, pleased to see that it was in good order. All it needed was a few minor repairs and a spraypaint but there was nothing that could be done this evening—she was too tired anyway. All Matilda wanted to do now was pack up her things and head for her temporary home. Actually, all Matilda wanted to do was *leave* her things and head for home, but mindful of safety she reluctantly headed over to the pile of equipment. She splashed some water from her bottle onto her face and decided more desperate measures were needed. Taking off her hat, she filled it and sloshed it onto her head, closing her eyes in blessed relief as the water ran down her face and onto her shoulders. Feeling the sting of cold on her reddened face and catching her breath, Matilda delighted in a shiver for a moment, before the sun caught up.

'Matilda.' The familiar voice made her jump. She'd been so sure she was alone, but here she was, soaked to the skin at her own doing, face smeared with mud, squinting into the low sunlight at the forebidding outline of Dante. 'I startled you. I'm sorry to barge in.'

'Not at all!' She shook her head and tried to look not remotely startled. 'It's your garden after all—I was just packing up.' Brutally aware of the mess she looked and with two nipples sticking out of her soaking top, thanks to the halflitre of water she'd just poured over herself, Matilda busied herself clearing up her tools as Dante came over.

'I thought I'd bring Alex to see the garden before she went to bed.' He was carrying her, which was just as well. It was rather more a demolition site than a garden

at the moment. Dante picked his way around the edge
and let Alex down on the one grassed area left—under
the willow tree. It was only patchily grassed, but at least
it was clean and dry—and given that the little girl was
dressed in her nighty and had clearly had her bedtime
bath, it was just as well. Matilda gave up in pretending
to look at her tools and watched him as he came over.
He was wearing shorts and runners—and no socks,
which just accentuated the lean, muscular length of his
brown calves. His whole body seemed incredibly toned,
actually—and Matilda momentary wondered how. He
didn't seem the type for a gym and he spent an immod-
erate time at the office.

'Hi, Alex.' Matilda smiled at the little girl, not
remotely fazed by the lack of her response, just enchanted by her beauty. 'I know it looks a terrible mess
now, but in a few days it will look wonderful.'

Alex didn't even appear to be looking—her eyes
stared fixedly ahead. A little rigid figure, she stood quite
still as Matilda chatted happily to her, explaining what
was going to happen over the next few days, pointing
out where the water features would be, the sand pit and
the enchanted castle.

'You've got a lot done today,' Dante observed. 'What
happens now?'

'The boring stuff,' Matilda answered. 'I've got the
plumber and electrician coming tomorrow and then the
concreters, but once all that's out the way, hopefully it
will start to take shape a bit.' And though she longed to
ask about his day, longed to extend the conversation just
a touch longer, deliberately she held back, determined

that it must be Dante who came to her now—she'd already been embarrassed enough. But the silence was excruciating as they stood there, and it was actually a relief when Dante headed over to his daughter and went to pick her up.

'Time for bed, little lady.' Something twisted inside Matilda at the tenderness in his voice, the strong gentle arms that lowered to lift his daughter. But Alex resisted, letting out a furious squeal that pierced the quiet early evening air, arching her back, her little hands curling into fists. Matilda's eyes widened at the fury that erupted in the little girl, stunned to witness the change in this silent, still, child. But clearly used to this kind of response, Dante was way too quick for Alex, gently but firmly taking her wrists and guiding her hands to her sides.

'No!' he said firmly. 'No hitting.'

With a mixture of tenderness and strength he picked Alex up, clasping her furious, resisting body to his chest, utterly ignoring the shrill screams, just holding her ever tighter. Finally she seemed to calm, the screams, the fury abating until finally Dante smiled wryly as he caught Matilda's shocked eyes. 'Believe it or not, I think you just received a compliment. Normally I don't have to even ask to bring her in from the garden. Perhaps she is going to like it after all.'

Two compliments even! Matilda thought to herself. Was Dante actually saying he liked her plans as well?

'I'll take her inside and get her to bed.' Matilda gazed at the little girl, now resting in her father's arms. Not a trace of the angry outburst of only moments before remained, her dark eyes staring blankly across the wilderness of the garden. 'Are you finishing up?'

'Soon.' Matilda nodded. 'I'm just going to pack my things.'

'You're welcome to come over for dinner…'

'No, thanks!' Matilda said, and she didn't offer an explanation, didn't elaborate at all, just turned her back and started to pack up her things.

'It's no trouble,' Dante pushed, but still she didn't turn around, determined not to give him the satisfaction of drawing her in just to reject her again, just to change his mind or hurt her with cruel words. 'I just warm the meal up tonight. Janet has her Alcoholics Anonymous meetings on Mondays and Thursdays.'

'But she said she had…' Matilda swung around then snapped her mouth closed, furious with herself for responding.

'Everyone has their secrets, remember.' Dante shrugged then gave her the benefit of a very wicked smile. 'Come,' he offered again.

'No,' Matilda countered. This time she didn't even bother to be polite, just turned her back on him and started to sort out her things, only letting out the breath she had been holding when, after the longest time, she heard the click of the gate closing. Alex didn't just have her father's eyes, Matilda realised, she had his personality, too. They shared the same dark, lonely existence, cruelly, capriciously striking out at anyone they assumed was getting too close, yet somehow drawing them in all the same, somehow managing to be forgiven.

* * *

A cold shower mightn't be so bad, Matilda attempted to convince herself as she gingerly held her fingers under the jets. All day she'd been boiling, all day she'd longed to cool down—but the trouble with her line of work was that there was absolutely no chance of a quick dart in the shower. Her hair was stiff with dust, her fingers black from the soil, her skin almost as dark as Dante's.

Biting down on her lip, Matilda dived into the shower, yelping as the icy water hit her. Forcing herself to put her head under, she frantically rubbed in shampoo, praying that in a moment she'd acclimatise, that the freezing water might actually merely be cool after a couple of minutes' more torture. Only it wasn't. Her misery lasted long after she'd turned the beastly taps off and wrapped a towel around her, her poorly rinsed hair causing a river of stinging of water to hit her eyes. Shivering and cursing like the navvy Katrina had hoped for, Matilda groped for the door handle, wrenching it open and storming head first into a wall of flesh.

'When were you going to tell me?' Dante demanded. 'I could hear you screaming…'

Matilda stood in shook. 'Are you spying on me?' She felt embarrassed and enraged. Her bloodshot, stinging eyes focused on the walkie-talkie he was holding in his hand.

'It's a child monitor,' he explained with infinite patience, as if she were some sort of mentally unhinged person he was talking down from the roof. But she could see the tiny twitch on his lips, knew that inside he was laughing at her, her misery, her embarrassment increasing as he carried on talking. 'Janet left a note, telling me about the water. I just read it, so will you, please, collect your belongings so that I can help you bring your things over.'

'There's really no need for that,' Matilda insisted, feeling horribly exposed and vulnerable and also somewhat deflated that even standing before him, her body drenched, clearly naked under a towel, she didn't move him at all. 'I've got a plumber coming tomorrow…'

'Matilda.' He gave a weary sigh. 'My daughter is asleep in the house alone so could you, please, just…?' He faltered for just a fraction of a second, telling her in that fraction of time that she had been wrong—that Dante was very aware of her near-nakedness. She clutched the towel tighter around her, scuffed the floor with her dripping foot as immediately he continued. 'Get dressed, Matilda,' he said gruffly. 'I'll come back for your things later.'

Which really didn't leave her much choice.

CHAPTER SIX

IT WAS a very shy, rather humble Matilda that joined Dante at the heavy wooden table that was the centrepiece of his impressive al fresco area, the beastly child monitor blinking at her on the table as she approached, her face darkening to purple as she realised she'd practically accused the man of stalking her. She braced herself for a few harsh words Dante-style but instead he poured an indecent amount of wine into her glass then pushed it across the table to her.

'Is red OK?'

'Marvellous,' Matilda lied, taking a tentative sip, surprised to find that this particular red actually was OK, warming her from the inside out. Holding the massive glass in her pale hand, she stared at the dark liquid, anything rather than look at him, and started a touch when the intercom crackled loudly.

'Static,' Dante explained, pressing a button. 'Someone down the road mowing their lawn or drying their hair. I just change the channel, see.'

'Oh.'

'You don't have any experience with children, do you?'

'None,' Matilda answered. 'I mean, none at all. Well apart from my friend, Sally…'

'She has a baby?'

'No.' Matilda gave a pale smile. 'But she's thought that she might be pregnant a couple of times.'

He actually laughed, and it sounded glorious, a deep rich sound, his white teeth flashing. Matilda was amazed after her exquisite discomfort of only a moment ago to find herself actually laughing, too, her pleasure increasing as Dante gave a little bit more, actually revealed a piece of himself, only not with the impassive voice he had used before but with genuine warmth and emotion, his face softer somehow, his voice warmer as this inaccessible man let her in a touch, allowed her to glimpse another dimension to his complex nature.

'Until Alex was born, apart from on television, I don't think I'd ever seen a newborn.' He frowned, as if examining that thought for the first time. 'No, I'm sure I hadn't. My mother was the youngest of seven children. All my cousins were older and I, too, was the youngest—very spoiled!'

'I can imagine.' Matilda rolled her eyes, but her smile remained as Dante continued.

'Then this tiny person appeared and suddenly I am supposed to know.' He spread his hands expressively, but words clearly failed him.

'I'd be terrified,' Matilda admitted.

'I was,' Dante stated. 'Still am, most of the time.'

Her smile faded, seeing him now not as the man that moved her but as the single father he was, trying yet knowing she was failing to fathom the enormity of the task that had been so squarely placed on his shoulders.

'It must be hard.'

'It is.' Dante nodded and didn't sweeten it with the usual superlatives that generally followed such a statement, didn't smile and eagerly nod that it was more than worth it, or the best thing he'd ever done in his life. He just stared back at her for the longest time, before continuing, 'I have a big trial starting next week, but once that it is out of the way, I need to make a decision.'

'Whether to move back to Italy?'

Dante nodded. 'Every doctor I have consulted tells me that Alex needs a routine, that she needs a solid home base—at the moment I am having trouble providing that. Katrina is only too willing to help, but...' He hesitated and took a long sip of his drink. Matilda held her breath, willing him to continue, to glean a little more insight into the problems he faced. 'She wants to keep Jasmine alive, doesn't want anything that might detract from her daughter's memory, which is understandable, of course, only sometimes...'

'It's a bit much?' Matilda tentatively offered, relieved when he didn't frown back at her, relieved that maybe she understood just a little of what he was feeling.

'Much too much,' Dante agreed, then terminated the conversation, standing up and gesturing. 'I will show you the guest room, it's already made up—then we can eat.'

'I might just grab a sandwich or something when I get my things,' Matilda started, but Dante just ignored her, leading her through the house and upstairs, gesturing for her to be quiet as they tiptoed past Alex's room, before coming to a large door at the end of the hallway.

Clearly Dante's idea of a guest room differed from Matilda's somewhat—her version was a spare room with a bed and possibly an ironing board for good measure. But Dante's guests were clearly used to better. As he pushed open the door and she stepped inside, Matilda realised just how far she'd been relegated by Katrina. Till then the summerhouse had been more than OK, but it wasn't a patch on this! A massive king-sized bed made up with crisp white linen was the focus point of the fabulously spacious room, but rather than being pushed against the wall and sensibly facing a door, as most of the population would have done, instead it stood proudly in the middle, staring directly out of one of the massive windows Matilda had till now only glimpsed from the outside, offering a panoramic view of the bay. Matilda thought she must have died and gone to heaven—ruing every last minute she'd spent struggling on in the summerhouse when she could have been here!

'I won't sleep,' Matilda sighed dreamily, wandering over to the window and pressing her face against the glass, like a child staring into a toy-shop Christmas display. 'I'll spend the whole night watching the water and then I'll be too exhausted to do your garden. It's just divine…'

'And,' Dante said with a teasing dramatic note to his voice that Matilda had never heard before, 'it has running water.'

'You're kidding.' Matilda played along, liking the change in him, the funnier, more relaxed side of him she was slowly starting to witness.

'Not just that, but *hot* running water.' Dante smiled, sliding open the *en suite* door as Matilda reluctantly peeled herself away from the view and padded over. 'See for yourself.'

The smile was wiped off her face as she stepped inside. Fabulous it might be but she couldn't possibly use it, her frantic eyes scanning the equally massive window for even a chink of a blind or curtain.

'No one can see.' Dante rolled his eyes at her expression.

'Apart from every passing sailor and the nightly ferry load on its way to Tasmania!' Matilda gulped.

'The windows are treated, I mean tinted,' Dante simultaneously explained and corrected himself. Even a couple of hours ago she'd have felt stupid or gauche, but his smile seemed genuine enough at least that Matilda was able to smile back. 'I promise that no one will see you.'

'Good.'

'Now that we've taken care of that, can we eat?'

This time she didn't even bother to argue.

Wandering back along the hallway, Dante put his fingers to his lips and pushed open Alex's door to check on his daughter. Matilda stood there as he crept inside. The little girl was lying with one skinny leg sticking out of between the bars of her cot, her tiny, angelic face relaxed in sleep. Matilda felt her heart go out to this beautiful child who had been through so, so much, a lump building in her throat as Dante slowly moved her leg back in then retrieved a sheet that had fallen from the cot and with supreme tenderness tucked it around Alex, gently stroking her shoulder as she stirred slightly.

But Matilda wasn't watching Alex any more. Instead, she was watching Dante, a sting of tears in her eyes as she glimpsed again his tenderness, slotted in another piece of the puzzle that enthralled her.

When he wasn't being superior or scathing he was actually incredibly nice.

Incredibly nice, Matilda thought a little later as Dante carried two steaming plates into the lounge room and they shared a casual dinner. And whether it was the wine or the mood, conversation came incredibly easily, so much so that when Matilda made a brief reference to her recent break-up, she didn't jump as if she'd been burnt when Dante asked what had gone wrong. She just gave a thoughtful shrug and pondered a moment before answering.

'I honestly don't know,' Matilda finally admitted. 'I don't really know when the problems started. For ages we were really happy. Edward's career was taking off, we were looking at houses and then all of a sudden we seemed to be arguing over everything. Nothing I did was ever right, from the way I dressed to the friends I had. It was as if nothing I did could make him happy.'

'So everything was perfect and then out of the blue arguments started?' Dante gave her a rather disbelieving frown as she nodded. 'It doesn't happen like that, Matilda,' Dante said. 'There is no such thing as perfect. There must have been something that irked, a warning that all was not OK—there always is.'

'How do you know?' Matilda asked, 'I mean how do you know all these things?'

'It's my job to know how people's minds work,'

Dante responded, but then softened it with a hint of personal insight. 'I was in a relationship too, Matilda. I do know that they are not all perfect!'

According to everyone, *his* had been, but Matilda didn't say it, not wanting to break the moment, liking this less reticent Dante she was seeing, actually enjoying talking to him. 'I supposed he always flirted when we were out and it annoyed me,' Matilda admitted. 'We'd go to business dinners and I didn't like the way he was with some of the women. I don't think I'm a jealous person, but if he was like that when I was there…' Her voice trailed off, embarrassed now at having said so much, but Dante just nodded, leaning back on the sofa. His stance was so incredibly nonjudgmental, inexplicably she wanted to continue, actually wanted to tell him how Edward had made her feel, wanted Dante to hear this and hoping maybe in return she'd hear about him, too. 'He wasn't cheating. But I wondered in years to come…'

'Probably.' Dante shrugged. 'No doubt when you'd just had a baby, or your work was busy and you were too tired to focus enough on him, not quite at your goal weight.' He must have registered her frown, her mouth opening then holding back a question that, despite the nature of this personal conversation, wasn't one she had any right to ask, but Dante answered it anyway. 'No, Matilda, I didn't have an affair, if that's what you are thinking. I like beautiful women as much as any man and, yes, at various times in our relationship Jasmine and I faced all of the things I've outlined, but I can truthfully say it would never have entered my head to look at another woman in that way. I wanted to fix our problems, Matilda, not add to them.'

And it was so refreshing to hear it, a completely different perspective, her doubts about opening up to him quashed now as she saw the last painful months through different eyes.

'In the end he spent so much time at work there really wasn't much room for anything else...'

'*Anything* else?' Dante asked, painfully direct, and Matilda took a gulp of her drink then nodded.

'You know, for months I've been going over and over it, wondering if I was just imagining things, if Edward was right, that it was my fault he couldn't...' She snapped her mouth closed. In an unguarded moment she'd revealed way, way more than she'd intended and she halted the conversation there, hoping that Dante would take the cue and do the same, but he was way too sharp.

'What was your fault?'

'Nothing.' Matilda's voice was high. 'Wasn't what I told you reason enough to end things?'

'Of course.'

Silence hung in the air. As understanding as Dante might have been, he certainly couldn't help her with the rest. There was no way she could go there, the words that had been said agony to repeat even to herself. It was none of his damn business anyway.

'You know, people like Edward normally don't respond too well to their own failings—they'd rather make you feel like shit than even consider that they had a problem.' His voice was deep and unusually gentle, and though she couldn't bring herself to look at him she could feel his eyes on her. His insight floored her. She felt transparent, as if somehow he had seen into the deepest, darkest part of her and somehow shed light on it, somehow pried open the lid on her shame. And it was madness, sheer madness that she wanted to open it up more, to let out the pain that was curled up inside there…to share it with Dante.

'He said that it was my fault…' Matilda gagged on the words, screwed her eyes closed, as somehow she told him, told him what she hadn't been able to tell even some of her closest friends. 'That maybe if I was more interesting, made a bit more effort, that he wouldn't look at other women, that he wouldn't have…' She couldn't go there, couldn't tell him everything, she could feel the icy chill of perspiration between her breasts, could feel her neck and her face darkening in the shame of the harsh, cruel words that had been uttered.

'I would imagine that it's incredibly difficult to be amazing in bed when you've been ignored all evening!' Her closed eyes snapped open, her mouth gaping as Dante, as direct as ever, got straight to the point. 'I would think it would be impossible, in fact, to give completely of yourself when you're wondering who he's really holding—whether it's the woman in his arms or the one you caught him chatting to at the bar earlier.'

And she hadn't anticipated crying, but as his words tore through her only then did she truly acknowledge the pain, the pain that had been there for so long now, the bitter aftermath that had lingered long after she'd moved out and moved on with her life. But they were quiet tears, no sobs, no real outward display of emotion other than the salty rivers that ran down her smeared cheeks, stinging her reddened face as Dante gently spoke on, almost hitting the mark but not quite. She'd revealed so much to him, but her ultimate shame was still locked inside.

'It was him with the problem, not you.' His accent was thick.

'He said the same thing—the other way around, of course.' Matilda sniffed. 'I guess it's a matter of opinion who's right! I spent the last few months trying to get back what we'd once had, trying to make it work, but in the end…' She shook her head, unwilling now to go on, the last painful rows still too raw for shared introspection. Thankfully Dante sensed it, offering her another drink from the bottle they'd practically finished, but Matilda declined. 'What about you?'

'Me?' Dante frowned.

'What about your relationship?' Matilda ventured.

'What about it?'

'You said that it wasn't perfect…'

'No.' Dante shook his head.

'You did,' Matilda insisted.

'I said that I knew that they were not *all* perfect—it doesn't mean I was referring to mine.'

Matilda knew he was lying and she also knew that he was closing the subject, yet she refused to leave it there. She'd revealed so much of herself, had felt close to a man for the first time in ages and didn't want it to end like this, didn't want Dante to shut her out all over again.

'You said that you wanted to fix your problems, Dante,' Matilda quoted softly. 'What were they?'

'Does it matter now?' Dante asked, swilling the wine around his glass and refusing to look at her. 'As you said, there are always two sides—is it fair to give mine when Jasmine isn't here to give hers?'

'I think so,' Matilda breathed, chewing on her bottom lip. And even if her voice was tentative, she reeled at her boldness, laid her heart on the line a little bit more, bracing herself for pain as she did so. 'If you want to get close to someone then you have to give a bit of yourself—even the bad bits.'

'And you want to get close?'

He did look at her this time, and she stared back transfixed, a tiny nervous nod affirming her want. 'Tell me about you, how you're feeling…'

'Which part of hell do you want to visit?'

She didn't flinch, didn't say anything, just stared back, watching as slowly he placed his glass on the table. His elbows on his knees, he raked a hand through his hair and so palpable was his pain Matilda was sure if she lifted her hand she'd be able to reach out and touch it. She held her breath as finally he looked up and stared at her for the longest time before speaking.

'Always there is…' He didn't get to start, let alone finish. A piercing scream from the intercom made them both jump. He picked up the intercom, which had been placed on the coffee table, and stood up. 'I have to go to her and then I think I'll head to bed, I've got a pile of paperwork to read. 'Night, Matilda.'

'Let me help with her…'

'She doesn't like strangers.' The shutters were up, his

black eyes dismissing her, the fragile closeness they had so nearly created evaporating in that instant.

'Dante…' Matilda called, but he wasn't listening, her words falling on his departing back as he closed the door behind him. 'Don't make me one.'

CHAPTER SEVEN

PREDICTABLY, Katrina had a plumber screeching up the driveway within seconds of Dante's chopper lifting off the smooth lawn, and Matilda could almost envisage her bags being moved yet again, but quietly hoped for a miracle. And it wasn't all about Dante. Waking up to the most glorious sunrise, stretching like a lazy cat in the scrummy bed, as superficial as it might be, Matilda was terribly reluctant to leave her very nice surroundings.

'White ants!' Katrina almost choked on her Earl Grey as the plumber she had summoned popped his head around the kitchen door and Matilda smothered a smile as she loaded a tray with coffee to take out to the workers for their break. 'Well, surely you can replace the water system and then we'll get the place treated once…' She managed to stop herself from saying it, but the unspoken words hung in the air and Matilda took great interest in filling up the sugar bowl as Katrina paused and then, rather more carefully, spoke on. 'Just sort out the water, please. It doesn't all have to be done today.'

'Can't do, I'm afraid,' he said cheerfully. 'The wall's

not stable enough to hold a new system. The place needs to be treated and then some of the walls will have to be replaced—it's going to be a big job.'

It wasn't the only big job the next couple of days un-earthed.

Katrina practically moved into Dante's, appearing long before he went to work and staying well into the night when Dante finally got home—not that Matilda really noticed. All her energies were taken up with the garden—her efficient start to the job but a distant memory as problems compounded problems. The glorious willow tree had roots that weren't quite as wondrous, thwarting Matilda's carefully lain plans at each and every turn. And a rather unproductive day followed by a floodlit late night were spent with the plumber and electrician, trying to find a suitable spot to lay the pipes for the water features. Then, just when that was taken care of, Matilda awoke to the news that, despite her inspection, the white ants had migrated from the summerhouse to the rear wall of the fence, which would set things back yet another day while it was ripped out and replaced. More skips delivered, more delays ensuing, and by the time she dragged herself back to the house, all Matilda could manage was a warmed-up meal and a very weary goodnight as, drooping with exhaustion, she headed off for bed.

Still as the week drew to a close, if not order then at least a semblance of control had been restored. Finally the pipes were laid, the electricity was on and the garden that had till now merely lived in her mind could actually start to emerge.

'I think we must have a mole on steroids,' Dante quipped, eyeing the mounds of earth that littered the area, and his easy humour bought the first smile in a long time to Matilda's tense face as he wandered in with Alex late one evening to check on the progress. 'I hear things haven't gone exactly to plan.'

'On the contrary,' Matilda replied. 'Things have gone exactly to plan—there's always a disaster waiting to happen with this kind of work. But I think we're finally under control.'

'Will you be joining us for dinner?'

'Us?' Matilda checked, because Alex was clearly ready for bed.

'Katrina and Hugh have come over—I should give Janet the numbers.'

'No, thanks.' Matilda shook her head but didn't elaborate, didn't make up an excuse or reason.

'I'm sorry I haven't been over.' Dante switched Alex to his other hip. 'My trial preparation has taken up a lot of time, things have been busy—'

'Tell me about it,' Matilda said, rolling her eyes.

'I'm sure that I'd bore you to death,' Dante responded, completely missing the point. But somehow the language barrier actually worked in their favour for once, the tiny misunderstanding opening a door, pushing the stilted, polite conversation way beyond the intentions of either participant. 'Are you really interested?'

'Very,' Matilda responded. 'Completely unqualified, of course, but terribly interested.'

'But you know that I cannot discuss it with you.'

'I know,' Matilda answered. 'I mean, at the end of the

day, the barrister mulling over his case with the gardener…'

'I cannot discuss it with *anyone*,' Dante broke in, and she watched as his eyes closed in shuttered regret, felt again the weight of responsibility that rode on his broad shoulders and ached to soothe him.

'I know,' Matilda said softly, then gave him a little spontaneous nudge. 'Well, I don't *know* exactly, but I have got pay TV.' She smiled at his frown. 'I've paced the courtroom floor with the best of them, and from what I've gleaned you're allowed to talk in general terms.'

'You're crazy.' Dante laughed, his palpable tension momentarily lifting, but the shrill of his mobile broke the moment. Matilda watched as he juggled his daughter and flicked out his mobile, watched the vivid concentration on his face, the turn of his back telling her that this call was important. She reacted as anyone would have, held out her arms and offered to take his daughter, lifting the little girl into her arms, hardly registering the surprise on Dante's face as he barked his orders into the phone.

'She went to you!'

A full fifteen minutes had passed. Fifteen minutes of Dante talking into the phone as Matilda at first held Alex but when she got a bit heavy, Matilda put her down, gathering the few exhausted, remaining daisies from under the willow, slitting the stalks with her thumb and making if not a daisy chain then at least a few links—chatting away to an uncommunicative Alex. But the little girl did appear to be watching at least and now Dante was kneeling down with them, staring open-mouthed at what Matilda considered was really a very normal scene.

'Sorry?' Matilda was trying to wrestle a very limp stalk into a very thin one.

'Alex actually went to you.' Dante's voice had a slightly incredulous note as he watched Alex take the small chain of daisies Matilda was offering.

'I'm really not that scary, Dante.' Matilda smiled.

'You don't understand. Alex doesn't go to anyone. You saw what she was like the other day when it was *me* trying to pick her up.'

'Maybe she's ready to start trusting a little again…' Matilda looked over at Dante and spoke over the little blonde head that was between them. Even though it was Alex she was talking about, they knew her words were meant for both. 'Maybe now she's done it once, it will be easier the next time.' For an age she stared at him, for an age he stared back, then his hands hovered towards his daughter, ready to pick her up and head for the house, ready to walk away yet again. But Matilda's voice halted him. 'Let her play for a few minutes. She's enjoying the flowers.' She was, her little fingers stroking the petals, concentration etched on her face, and for all the world she looked like any other little girl lost in a daydream. 'Talk to me, Dante,' Matilda said. 'You might surprise yourself and find that it helps.'

'I don't think so.'

'I do,' Matilda said firmly, watching as his gaze drifted to Alex, and finally after the longest time he spoke.

'Remember when we talked at the restaurant?' She could hear him choosing his words carefully. 'You asked if I ever regret winning and I said no?' Matilda nodded. 'I lied.'

'I know,' Matilda answered.

'Not professionally, of course.' Dante pondered, his accent a little more pronounced as his mind clearly wandered elsewhere. 'I always walk into a courtroom wanting to win, I wouldn't be there otherwise, but, yes, sometimes there is a feeling of…' He snapped his fingers in impatience as he tried to find the right word.

'Regret?' Matilda offered, and Dante shook his head.

'Unease,' he said. 'A sense of unease that I do my job so well.'

'There would have to be,' Matilda said carefully, knowing she couldn't push things, knowing she had to listen to the little information he was prepared to give.

'There is another side, too, though…' His eyes found and held hers and Matilda knew that what he was about to tell her was important. 'There are certain cases that matter more. Matter because…' He didn't continue, couldn't perhaps, so Matilda did it for him.

'Because if you won there would be no unease?' She watched the bob of his Adam's apple as he swallowed, knew she had guessed correctly, that Dante was telling her, as best he could, that the man he was defending was innocent and that this case, perhaps, mattered more than most.

'You'll win,' Matilda said assuredly, and Dante let out a tired sigh and gave a rather resigned smile, pulling himself up to go, clearly wondering why he'd bothered talking to her if that was the best she could come up with! 'You will—you always do,' Matilda said with absolute conviction. 'Your client couldn't have better representation.'

'Matilda,' Dante said with dry superiority, 'we're *not* talking about my client and, anyway, you have absolutely no idea what you're talking about.'

'Oh, but I do.' Her green eyes caught his as he reached out for his daughter.

'You know nothing about law,' Dante needlessly pointed out. 'You know nothing about—'

'Perhaps,' Matilda interrupted. 'But you've already told me what you're capable of, already told me that you can do it even if you don't believe…' She paused for a moment, remembering the rules, remembering that she had to keep it general. 'If I were in trouble, I mean.' She gave a cheeky grin. 'Suppose I *had* been caught taking those chocolates and assuming I could afford you…' She gave a tiny roll eye as her fantasy took on even more bizarre proportions. 'I'd want to walk into court with the best.'

'Am I the best for him, though?' He raked a hand through his jet hair and it was Dante who forgot to keep things general.

'Absolutely,' Matilda whispered. 'I'd want the best I could afford, Dante, but having you believe in me would mean a thousand times more. Think of what you've already achieved then imagine what you're capable of when you actually believe in someone.' A frown marred his brow, but it wasn't one of tension, more realization, and Matilda knew that she'd got through to him, knew that somehow she'd reassured him, maybe helped a little even. 'You're going to be fine,' Matilda said again, and this time he didn't bite back, this time he didn't shoot her down with some superior remark, just gave her a gentle nod of thanks.

'Time for bed, Alex,' Matilda said, holding her arms out to the little girl, and even though Alex didn't hold out her own arms, she didn't resist when Matilda picked her up and wandered with Dante to the gate.

'She likes you,' Dante said as he took a sleepy Alex from Matilda.

'I'm very easy to like,' Matilda answered.

'Very easy,' Dante said, only, unlike before, Matilda knew there were no double meanings or cruel euphemisms to mull over. As he walked away the echo of his words brought a warm glow to her tired, aching body.

Quite simply it was the nicest thing he'd ever said.

CHAPTER EIGHT

'I'M SORRY to have disturbed you.'

'It's fine.' Matilda attempted, struggling to sit up, slightly disorientated and extremely embarrassed that Dante had found her in the middle of the day, hot and filthy in nothing more than the skimpiest of shorts and a crop top, lying on a blanket with her eyes closed. Absolutely the *last* person she was expecting to see at this hour, he was dressed in his inevitable dark suit, but there was a slightly more relaxed stance to him. He held a brown paper bag in one hand and he didn't look in his usual rush—his usually perfectly knotted tie was loosened, the top button of his shirt undone. But his dark eyes were shielded with sunglasses making his closed expression even more unreadable if that were possible.

'You've done a lot.'

'It's getting there.' Matilda nodded. 'And if I keep going at full speed, I could still be done by early next week.'

He didn't say a word, he didn't have to. Just a tiny questioning lift of his eyebrow from behind his dark glasses was enough for Matilda.

'I am allowed to take a break,' Matilda retorted.

'I didn't say anything!'

'You might not have *said* it but I certainly *heard* it. I am allowed to take a break, Dante. For your information, I've been working since first light this morning—apart from a coffee at ten I haven't stopped.'

'You don't have to justify yourself to me.'

'No, I don't.' Matilda agreed.

'How you organise your time is entirely your business. It's just…' His voice faded for a moment, a hint of a very unusual smile dusting across his face. 'I think I must be in the wrong job. "Flat out" for me is back-to-back meetings, endless phone calls, figures, whereas the twice I've seen you work, you're either taking an impromptu shower with a water bottle or dozing under a tree.' She opened her mouth to set him straight, but Dante spoke over her. 'I am not criticising you, I can see for myself the hours of work you have done. For once I was not even being sarcastic—I really was thinking back there when I saw you that I am in the wrong job!'

'You are.' Matilda smiled, the wind taken out of her sails by his niceness. 'And for the record, I wasn't dozing.'

'Matilda, don't try and tell me that you weren't asleep. You didn't even hear me come over. You were lying on your back with your eyes closed.'

'I was meditating,' Matilda said and seeing the disbelieving look on his face she elaborated further. 'I did hear you come over, I just…' It was Matilda's voice fading now, wondering how she could explain to him that in her deeply relaxed state she had somehow discounted the information.

'Just what?'

'I didn't hold onto the thought.'

'You've lost me.' He shook his head as if to clear it. 'You're really telling me that you weren't asleep!'

'That's right—I often meditate when I'm working, that's where I get my best ideas. You should try it,' she added.

'I have enough trouble getting to sleep at one in the morning, let alone in the middle of the day.'

'My point exactly,' Matilda said triumphantly. 'I've already told you that I wasn't asleep. You're very quick to throw scorn, but sometimes the best way to find the answer to a question is to stop looking for it.'

'Perhaps.' Dante gave a dismissive shrug. 'But for now I'll stick with the usual methods. I actually came to see if you wanted some lunch.' Before she could shake her head, before she could come up with an excuse as to why she didn't want to go over and eat with Katrina, Dante held out the paper bag he was holding. 'I bought some rolls from the deli.'

'The deli?'

'Why does that surprise you?'

'I don't know,' Matilda admitted, her neck starting to ache from staring up, feeling at a distinct disadvantage as Dante hovered over her. Wiggling over, she patted the blanket for him to sit beside her. 'It just does. How come you're home?'

'I live here,' Dante quipped, but he *did* sit down beside her, pulling the rolls out of the bag and offering one to her. 'I've spent the entire morning trying to read an important, complicated document relating to the case and haven't got past the second page. My new secretary cannot distinguish between urgent and urgent yet.'

'I don't understand.'

'Invariably anyone who wants to speak with me says that it is urgent—but she puts them all through, then I get waylaid. I decided to follow your business methods, they seem to be working for you.'

'What method?' Matilda gasped. 'I didn't know I had one!'

'Turning the phone off and disappearing. Katrina is out with Alex today. I thought there was more chance of actually getting some work done if I just came home, but first I must have some lunch.'

'I didn't hear the chopper!'

'I drove,' Dante said, 'and it was nice.' They ate in amicable silence until Dante spoiled it, his words almost causing her to choke on her chicken and avocado roll. 'I was thinking about you.'

'Me?'

'And how much I enjoy talking to you.' He took off his dark glasses and smiled a lazy smile, utterly comfortable in his own skin as Matilda squirmed inside hers, wriggling her bare feet in the moss and staring at her toes. 'And you're right, it's nice to take a moment to relax.'

Relaxed certainly wasn't how Matilda would describe herself now. He was so close that if she moved her leg an inch they'd be touching, if his face came a fraction closer she knew they'd be kissing. Desire coursed through her as it had when she'd cut herself, only this time Dante didn't seem to be pulling back, this time he was facing her head on. It was Matilda who turned abruptly away, terrified he'd read the naked lust in her eyes. She took a long drink from her water bottle then, blowing her fringe skywards and trying to keep her voice normal, determined not to make a fool of herself again, to be absolutely sure she wasn't misreading things, she said, 'You should try meditating if you want to be relaxed.'

'It wouldn't work,' Dante dismissed.

'It won't if that's your attitude…' She could feel the atmosphere sizzling between them, knew that if she said what was on her mind then she'd be crossing a line, playing the most dangerous of dangerous games. 'Try it,' she breathed, her eyes daring him to join her. 'Why don't you lie back and try it now?'

'Now?' Dante checked, a dangerous warning glint in his eyes, which she heeded, but it only excited her more.

'Now,' Matilda affirmed. 'Just lie back.'

'Then what?' Dante's impatient voice demanded instruction as, impossibly tense, he lay back.

'You close your eyes and just breathe,' Matilda said, her head turning to face him, her own breath catching in her throat as she gazed at his strong profile. She'd been right with her very first assessment of Dante. He was astonishingly beautiful—his eyes were closed and black, surprisingly long lashes spiked downwards onto indigo smudges of exhaustion. His nose was chiselled straight, so straight and so absolutely in proportion to the rest of his features she could almost imagine some LA cosmetic surgeon downing his tools in protest as he surveyed the landscape of Dante Costello's flawless face.

Flawless.

A perfectionist might point out that he hadn't shaved, but the stubble that ghosted his strong jaw, merely accentuated things: a shiver of masculinity stirring beneath the surface; a glimpse of what he might look like in the intimate dawn of morning. His full mouth was the only softening feature, but even that was set in grim tension as he lay there.

'You have to relax,' Matilda said, her words a contradiction because her whole body lay rigid beside him, her own breath coming in short, irregular bursts. Even her words were stilted, coming in short breathy sentences as they struggled through her vocal cords. 'Use your stomach muscles and breathe in through your nose and out through your mouth.'

'What?' One eye peeped open.

'Abdominal breathing,' she explained, but from the two vertical lines appearing over the bridge of his nose Matilda knew she was talking to the hopelessly unconverted.

'You don't move your chest,' Matilda explained. 'Remember when Alex was a baby and you watched her sleep?'

The frown faded a touch, a small smile lifting one edge of his mouth.

'Babies know how to relax,' Matilda said. 'They instinctively *know* how to breathe properly.'

'Like this?' Dante asked, dragging in air, and Matilda watched as he struggled with the concept. His stomach was moving but so too was his chest.

'Almost. Look, I'll help you. Just push against my hand.' Sitting up slightly, she instinctively moved to correct him. She'd shown this to numerous friends, knew how to show him simply, but her movements were hesitant, her hand tentative as it reached out towards him, hovered over the flat plane of his stomach, knowing, *knowing* where this could lead, wanting to pull back, to end this dangerous game, but curiously excited to start, to touch him, to feel him…

Her hand still hovered over his stomach but it was just too much, too intimate, and instead she placed her other hand on his chest, feeling the warmth of his skin through his shirt, feeing the breath still in him. Her fingers ached, literally ached to move his loosened tie, to creep between the buttons and feel his skin against hers. But she pushed away that thought, concentrated instead on keeping her voice even as she delivered her instructions. 'My hand shouldn't move. Breathe in through your nose, using your stomach, and then out through your mouth—here.' It seemed more appropriate now to touch his stomach than when the initial contact had been made, and she gently brushed her hand along on his stomach, felt the heavy leather of his belt, the coolness of his buckle and the silk of his trousers. Her whole body rippled with a lust she had never experienced—never thought she could experience—and she herself had engineered it because she wanted to be closer to him. More than that she didn't know, just knew she couldn't take a minute more of the crazy feelings that had been going on. 'Push against my hand,' Matilda said, 'and then hold your breath before letting out it. And just let your mind wander.'

For a second, two perhaps, he did. She felt him relax a touch beneath her, but it was fleeting, resistance rushing back in, his hand pushing hers away, Dante turning now to face her.

'Show me,' he said.

'I don't want to.' Matilda shook her head, knew she was incapable of going back to that tranquil place with Dante so close, but he was insistent. 'If it's so easy to do, prove it.'

Lying on her back Matilda closed her eyes, willed herself calm, trying to force herself to relax. But she could feel the tension in her hands and she drew on her reserves, dragged in the fragrant air, holding it, holding it and slowly letting it out, could feel his eyes watching her body move. And amazingly it happened. Somehow she did wander to that place she visited so often, but it was a different journey altogether, one she had never taken before. With every breath she sank deeper and yet her desire grew, visualising, willing his hands to touch her, for him to rest his palm on her stomach, fleeting, decadent thoughts that were hers only, her limbs heavy against the damp grass, the erotic thought of him near her stomach tightening with the anticipation of a touch that might never come.

His breath on her face caught her unawares. Her mind hadn't ever been so attuned to her body. She had been so sure his eyes had been there, the shiver of his breath on her cheeks was a shock, but even as her mind processed the sensation it was experiencing a new one—his mouth, pressing lightly on hers, so soft if it hadn't have been him it would surely have been imperceptible, could almost have been put down to imagination for nowhere else did he touch her. The sun blocked out as he hovered over her, her eyes still closed as she bliss-fully attuned to the feel of his lips lightly on hers until it wasn't enough. He was waiting for her bidding, she instinctively knew that. She could smell the bitter orange and bergamot undertones of his cologne, his breath mingling with hers, and after seconds that seemed to drag for ever she gave him her consent with her mouth, pressed her own lips into his.

The greeting was acknowledged by the reward of his cool tongue parting her lips, slipping inside, and that de-licious taste of him, the intimate feel of his mouth inside hers, his tongue languorously capturing hers, playing a slow teasing game, long strokes that made her want more, countered by a tiny feather-light stroke on the tip of her tongue and then a gentle sucking as he dragged her deeper into him. And it was the most erotic of kisses yet the most frustrating, because still nowhere else did he touch her. Only their mouths were touching, only their mouths in contact, and she wanted more, her body arching, trying to convey her needs. But he misread them, just kissed her ever on, till she burnt for more, lit-erally ached for more, and only then did he give it, but in a selfish, measured dose.

The hand that she desired, that she anticipated around her waist to pull her towards him, instead lay on the soft inner flesh of her thigh, and the impact was as acute as if he'd struck her with a branding iron. It was her thigh, for heaven's sake, Matilda mentally begged, just a few square inches of flesh, and it wasn't even moving, but it was intimate, it was so damned intimate that it was surely wrong to be lying here beneath him now. She wished his hand would move, but it didn't. Instead, it pressed harder, almost imperceptibly at first but slowly she could feel his fingers digging into the tender flesh. Her breath in his mouth was coming faster now, and just as she went to push him away, to move his hand to safer ground, Dante was the one who stopped. Propped up on his elbow, she could feel him gazing down at her and she lay there vulnerable, reluctant to open her eyes, terrified, excited at the same time, wondering what he would do next.

'How else?' His words confused her, questions inappropriate now, his touch what she needed, not the mind games he played. 'How else did Edward hurt you?'

'I've told you,' Matilda gulped, screwing her eyes closed tighter wishing he would just leave it, and sure he knew she was lying.

'Not all of it,' Dante said, his finger trailing along her arm as she spoke, the nub of his finger lingering on her radial pulse, like some perverse lie detector as he dragged her secrets out. 'Was *that* supposed to be your fault, too?'

'I didn't help,' Matilda croaked, her eyes still screwed closed, unable to look at him as she revealed her shame. 'Edward said that maybe if I dressed up…'

'Would he want you now?' Dante breathed, interrupting her, confusing her again. 'All messed up, in your work clothes?'

'Of course not,' Matilda started, but her voice trailed off, not sure what he was getting at. Her body was still throbbing with desire, an argument starting somewhere deep within, because Dante had wanted her, hadn't he?

Doubt was starting to ping in, her eyes snapping open, terrified that he was laughing at her, dreading being humiliated again. But in one movement he grabbed her wrist, rammed her tense hand between his legs. She pulled back as if she'd been scalded, the strength of his erection shocking her, the feel of him in her hand terrifying. But Dante pulled her hand back, holding it there till the fear abated, till the arousal that had always been there stirred again.

'You make me feel like this, *mi cora*.'

She could feel him growing in her palm, feel a trickle of sweat between her breasts as he swelled harder beneath her touch, a bubble of moisture between her legs as his fingers crept up her T-shirt now, tiny, delicate strokes as he inched up slowly further, and it had gone too far, way, way too far. She murmured her protest, attempted to halt things, but he kissed her harder, captured her protest with his tongue and silenced it. She could feel the fleshy pad of his index finger circling her aching nipple as he held the soft plumpness of her bosom in his palm. Only now did his lips release hers. Any sooner and she would have begged him to stop, would have halted things.

But now she was putty in his skilled hands, pliable, warm, willing to move, to let him do with her what he wanted, and, oh, how he did—kissing the pulse leaping in her throat as she wriggled out of her top. The second her breasts were free, his tongue paid them the attention they deserved, tender attention, kissing the swollen, needy tips in turn, his finger retracing his steps, working downwards now. Her stomach tightened in renewed tension as he slid down the zip of her shorts, but for the first time since contact he spoke, the liquid deep tones of his voice not breaking the spell but somehow deepening it.

'Don't hold onto those thoughts, *bella*, just let them come and go.' Repeating the words she had said to him, but with entirely different meaning this time. And she tried, really tried to just relax as his hand cupped her bottom and lifted her enough to slip off the shorts and knickers in one. But the movement erased what had been achieved, embarrassment flooding in as her flesh was exposed, her knees lifting instinctively and her hand moving down in a futile attempt to cover herself. Wanting to hide her body from Dante's gaze. She half expected his wrist to close around her hand, as Edward's had done, to roughly demand to return to where he had just been.

'Don't fight,' he ordered, but unlike Edward he was soothing her with words instead of touch. 'Don't think about that, just think about this.' His hand hovered over her stomach until she caught her breath. She wanted the contact again and he was very gently tracing tiny endless circles around the little hill of her abdomen as his lips dusted her cheeks. He was kissing away the salty tears that were spilling from her eyes with his other hand around her neck, massaging her hairline, yet still the hungry swell of him against her told Matilda how much he desired her. A barrage of sensations that could have been confusing but instead soothed, the panic that had momentarily engulfed her waned until she lay outstretched and acquiescent in his arms, thrumming with anticipation for all that he might yield.

'I'm going to touch you now.'

He was already touching her, his body was pressed

against her, his lips on her face, his erection jutting into her, but she knew what he meant, was grateful for the strange warning, shivering as his hand reached her damp intimate curls and gently stroked them, his lip capturing the nervous swallow in her throat as his fingers crept slowly deeper, the infinitely gentle strokes he had teased her with before almost rough in comparison to the tenderness he displayed now, gently circling, pressing. But what if she couldn't, what if she let him down? She felt herself tense but not in desire, that panic again creeping in as he slid a finger into her tight space, slid it in slowly, taking her dew and then back to where it was needed. His touch firmer, massaging away her fears and replacing them with need, as she quivered at his touch, uncurling under his masterful skill, his palm massaging her swollen mound, over and over, his fingers gliding in and out, patience in every movement. She opened her eyes once, drunk on lust, moaning at the blissful warmth that fired her, and she saw his eyes smiling down at her, not a trace of superiority in them, just desire.

'Matilda.' It was Dante's voice that was breathless now, *his* body pressing harder into hers. She'd been so indulgent in her own pleasure while he'd been so unselfish, but that he could be so aroused from just touching her was all the affirmation she needed. Bold, so bold now, it was Matilda making the move, wrestling with his heavy belt, unzipping him, pushing the silk of his boxers down and staring with animal lust at him, the swollen, angry tip almost explosive. And even if it was the most wanton, outrageous thing she had ever done, even if all there could be was this moment, she needed it, needed him deep, deep inside her. She wanted his weight on top of her and it was heaven as Dante pushed her down, his clothed body squeezing the breath out of her, strong knees parting her willing thighs. She could feel him nudging at her entrance and opened her legs a fraction more to accommodate him. Even before his heated length stabbed into her, her body was convulsing, her most intimate place wrapping around his, dragging him deeper with each quivering contraction of her orgasm as he moved within her.

'More!'

Her eyes opened. Breathless, speechless, she stared at him as still he moved within her. What did he mean more? She'd achieved more than she had ever thought possible—he'd already toppled her to climax.

'Give me more, Matilda.' He was pushing harder and now so was she. Now he was sliding over her, pressing her harder into the ground. But her body wanted to still, to recover from her orgasm, and she'd thought he'd been close, was sure he'd wanted her as much as she'd wanted him. For a second the doubts were back, the tiny dark voices that told her over and over she wasn't quite good enough, wasn't sexy enough, wasn't woman enough to please a man.

'Matilda,' Dante gasped. 'Come with me. I can't hold on—see what you do to me?'

He stared down at her and it was as if Dante was struggling to stay in control—and her body that had begged respite, mere moments before, rippled into delighted action as he ambushed her. Her legs wriggled free, wrapping themselves tightly around his hips, pulling him fiercely in, her fingers digging into the taut muscle of his buttocks. And she understood, understood then that she'd never truly let go, had merely glanced around the door of the place Dante was taking her to now.

'You're beautiful *bella*.' Over and over he said it. His chin was rough against her tender face, his breathing rapid and irregular, and she felt powerful now, felt his desire, his blatant need for her irrefutable. 'Dante…Dante.' Over and over she said. Pulling his shirt up, her hands ran over his back as her own frenzied mouth searched for comfort, sucking, licking the salty flesh of his chest,

'What you do to me!' Dante rasped. 'You sexy bitch…' His body his words were one unguarded paroxysm now, but so, too, was Matilda. She felt sexy, he *made* her sexy, her body responding to his debauched words, shivering as he spilled his precious nectar and she dragged it from him, convulsing around his length, dragging each delicious drop as if it was her right, as if it was hers to take, her whole body in rigid spasm, clinging to him as still somehow he moved, slower now, giving her all of him until, sated, exhausted, he collapsed on top of her before rolling onto his side, pulling her into his arms and welcoming her, back to a world that was more beautiful for what had taken place.

'You are so beautiful,' Dante drawled, then gave a small cough. 'Matilda, what I said just then…I mean, maybe I went too far…'

'Maybe I needed to hear it.' Matilda smiled. 'In fact, I think it's one of the nicest things anyone's ever said to me.'

He laughed—a real laugh—and it sounded so good. To see him relaxed, smiling, was like glimpsing somehow a different man, and all she knew was that she wanted more of this. He ran his hand over her warm, naked body and she squirmed with pleasure, not embarrassment, couldn't believe she was lying naked in his arms in the middle of the day and feeling only beautiful. 'At least we've answered your question.'

'What question?'

He kissed her very slowly, very tenderly before answering.

'It was Edward's problem, not yours.' He kissed the tip of her nose as his words sank in.

'Or you're just an amazing lover!'

'Oh, that, too.' Dante grinned.

'You know, sometimes people say things in an argument that they don't really mean.'

Matilda gazed up at him. 'Perhaps,' she said softly. 'Or in anger they find the courage to say what's really on their mind.'

The sun must have gone behind a cloud, because suddenly his face darkened, his body that had been so yielding, so in tune with hers stiffening, and Matilda wasn't sure if it was because of what she'd said or because he'd heard it first. The sound of tyres crunching on the gravel had them both jumping like scalded cats, suddenly aware of her lack of attire and Dante's trousers around his knees. She hated the intrusion, wanted so much to see him properly, the glimpse of his tumescence as he hastily pulled his trousers up and tucked himself in nowhere near enough for Matilda.

'Dante!' Katrina's voice pierced the still afternoon. Completely flustered, somehow Matilda managed to dress in record time, zipping up her shorts and almost falling over as she pulled on her boots, until, with her heart pounding, the footsteps drew closer and the gate was pushed open. Matilda did not even look over as Katrina approached and bluntly addressed Dante. 'I saw your car—what on earth are you doing home?'

'Trying to catch up on some reading,' Dante said casually, but it didn't wash with Katrina and after a long pause he elaborated. 'I thought I'd see how the garden was coming along before I shut myself away for the rest of the day. Where's Alex?'

Katrina didn't say anything at first, suspicious eyes swivelling from Dante to Matilda. 'Asleep in the car,' she finally said slowly. 'I was just going to carry her in.'

'I'll come and help,' Dante offered, but Katrina had already gone, walking out of the garden without a backward glance. Matilda stood with her cheeks flaming, her anxious eyes swinging to Dante, hoping for reassurance.

'Do you think she knew?'

'Of course not.' Dante shook his head but a muscle was pounding in his cheek, his hands balled into fists by his sides, and Matilda realised that Katrina's intrusion hadn't just wrecked the intimate moment—it was almost as if she'd erased it completely. 'Why on earth would she think there was anything between us?'

She truly wasn't sure if he was trying to reassure her, or was blatantly degrading her, but Matilda did a double-take, stunned at the change in him. Gone was the man who had so recently held her and in his place was the inaccessible man she had first encountered.

'Because maybe she guessed that we just made love.'

Matilda eyes glittered with tears, willing him to take it back, to perhaps realise the brutality of what he had just said, to offer some sort of apology. But Dante just stood there refusing to take it as she offered him an out from his rancid words. 'Because maybe she's noticed that over the last few days we've become close…'

'No.' His single word hurt her even more, if that were possible, his refusal to soften it cheapening her more than she'd thought possible.

'So what was that all about?' Matilda asked, gesturing to where they had lain, where he'd found her, held her, made love to her, forcing the confrontation, steeling herself to hear the confirmation of her worst fears. 'What just happened there, Dante?'

'Sex.' Black eyes stung her, a warning note in his voice telling her she'd crossed the line. His lips set in a rigid line as she shook her head, refused his take on the history they'd so recently created.

'It was more than that and you know it,' Matilda rasped, shocked by his callousness, reeling from the ferociousness of his sparse summing-up, yet refusing to buy it, because she knew there was more to him, had witnessed the real Dante only moments before, and all she knew was that she wanted him back. 'Dante, please, don't do this…' Matilda attempted, her hand reaching out for his arm, but he recoiled as if she was contaminated, shook her off as if she revolted him.

'Good sex, then,' came the elaboration she had foolishly hoped for, the bile at the back of her throat appropriate as he told her his poisonous truth. And it was

Matilda recoiling now, Matilda putting up the shutters and swearing she'd never let this man near her again.

'No, Dante, it wasn't.' This time she wasn't lying, wasn't denying what she felt. Looking into his cold, hard eyes, she told him the absolute truth. 'Good sex isn't just the act, Dante, it's about how you feel afterwards, and right now, I couldn't feel worse.' She knew he was about to walk off, knew that if she didn't say what was on her mind now then it would fester for ever, had learnt that much at least, so whether he was listening or not she chose to say what she felt. 'I don't know what your problem is, I don't know what it is that drives you to shut out something that could have been so good. Maybe you can justify it by saying that I'm not sophisticated enough to play by your rules, or that I don't hold a candle to your wife, but that's entirely your business. Frankly, I don't care any more.'

His only response was a blink, but she knew that she'd surprised him, knew that even as he shut her out further, right now a little of what she was saying was reaching him. It gave her the impetus to continue, the pain he'd inflicted more than enough to go round. 'I'm more sorry than you'll ever know for having *sex* with you, Dante, but, let's get one thing clear—I might have lost a bit of my pride here, but you just lost one helluva lot more…' It was Matilda who walked off, Matilda who headed to the house and left him standing in the garden. She refused to cry, just called her parting shot over her shoulder. 'You just lost me!'

CHAPTER NINE

HIS callousness, his emotional distancing after the intimacy they'd shared made the most painful of decisions relatively easy, made walking away from Dante about need rather than want. Because sharing his home, glimpsing his life and being shut out over and over was a torture that couldn't be sustained and gave Matilda the momentum to pick up the phone and call on every friend and colleague she could muster with a view to rapidly finishing the task she had committed herself to, and rapidly removing herself from this impossible situation she had allowed herself to fall into.

It was the most exhausting time of her life. Hanging the expense, more than happy to bill him, more than happy to pay for it herself even, Matilda ordered floodlights to enable her to work long into the warm nights, grateful for the soothing diversion of nature, grateful that by the time her aching body fell into bed at night, all she was capable of was rest, taking the respite of a dreamless, exhausted sleep while knowing the pain would surely come later.

* * *

'I can't believe what you've achieved.' Deep into a humid, oppressive Saturday evening, Hugh poured her a glass of champagne Matilda didn't want from the bottle he was holding, having wandered over from the al fresco area where the *family* had eaten a leisurely dinner. He was now staring in astonishment at the garden, which was almost complete, the sleeping beauty truly awoken, the overgrown wilderness a distant memory. In its place was a child's paradise—a maze of soft hedges, each leading to its own exciting end, soft turf underfoot and thousands of tiny fairy-lights adorning the massive willow—twinkling in the dusky light and bidding enchantment. 'What do you think, Katrina?'

'It's very nice.' Katrina's response wasn't exactly effusive, but Matilda couldn't have cared less. The only thing she needed to see her through was the knowledge that in less than twelve hours she'd be out of there, in less than twelve hours she could start to pick up the pieces of her life Dante had so readily shattered. 'Of course,' Katrina added, 'it's Alex's opinion that counts.'

Almost on cue, the gate opened and, as she had over the last couple of days whenever their paths had inadvertently crossed, Matilda didn't even look at Dante. Instead, she focused her attention on Alex, who walked tentatively alongside him, her tiny hand in his. She looked utterly adorable, dressed in cotton pyjamas and cute kitten slippers, newly washed blonde curls framed her pretty face. And as livid and as debased as Matilda felt, momentarily at least, it faded as she watched the little girl's reaction. Watched as her normally vacant eyes blinked in wonder as she actually surveyed the transformation, a smile breaking out on her serious face as Matilda flicked on a switch and the water features danced into life. It was like seeing the sun come out as a tiny gasp of wonder escaped Alex's lips. She moved forward, reached out and ran, *ran* as most children would have, but because it was Alex it was amazing.

'I think she likes it.' She could forgive Hugh's stilted words, because tears were running down his cheeks as he watched his granddaughter run through the water jets, and for that moment in time Matilda decided that the pain she'd endured had been worth it. To see this distant, reclusive child emerge from her shell, even if only for a moment, that her vision, her concept had actually reached this troubled, fractured child caused something good and pure to well deep inside her. Matilda's usual happiness, which had been stifled since Dante's rejection, bubbled to the surface again as she witnessed her work through the eyes of a child.

A child like Alex.

'Look!' Matilda's voice was an excited whisper. She crouched to Alex's level, as she had on the first day, taking her cautious hand as she had back then and beckoning Alex to new wonders as Katrina and Hugh wandered around to explore. 'Look what's here!' Parting the curtain of willow, Matilda led her inside the cool enclosure, the fairy-lights she had so carefully placed lighting the darkness and creating a cool, emerald oasis, an enchanted garden within a garden, a place for Alex to simply just be. But the innocent pleasure of the moment was broken as the leaves parted, as Dante stepped into the magical space and completely broke the spell.

'You could put engravings on the bark.' Matilda's voice was a monotone now as she addressed Dante, talking like a salesperson delivering her pitch. 'Or hang some mirrors and pictures, perhaps put down a blanket and have a crib for her dolls…'

'She loves it,' Dante broke in, the emotion that was usually so absent in his voice rolling in the distance as he sat down on the mossy ground, watching as his daughter stared up at the twinkling lights, her hands held in the air, fingers dancing along with them. 'It is the first time I have seen her happy in a long time.'

'Not so bad for a *stupido* garden?' Matilda said, and if she sounded bitter, she was: bitter for the way he had treated her; bitter for all they had lost. But because Alex was present, Matilda swallowed her resentment down, instead giving Dante the information he would need if the garden she had planted was to flourish. 'I've just got to clean up and attend to a few minor details tomorrow, but I'll be gone by lunchtime.'

'By lunchtime?' There was a tiny start to his voice, a frown creeping across his brow, which Matilda chose to ignore. 'I probably won't catch up with you tomorrow, but I'll write up some instructions for your gardener and run through a few things with you now. Know that the whole garden will improve with time.' Picking at some moss on the ground, Matilda continued, 'Every day you should see some changes. The paths are littered with wild seeds—buttercups, daisies, clover— so you shouldn't mow too often…'

'Matilda?'

'There are no sharp edges.' Ignoring him, she continued, trying to get through her summing-up, knowing this was one job she wouldn't be following up, knowing she was seeing it for the last time. 'And no plants that can hurt, no thorns that could scratch, nothing that might sting—she should be perfectly safe here. This garden is what you make of it—you could pick marigold leaves with Alex to add to your salad at night—'

'Matilda, we need to talk,' he interrupted again, one hand creeping across the ground to capture hers. But she pulled away, determined to see this last bit through with whatever dignity she could muster, yet unable to stop herself from looking at him for what was surely going to be the last time. Her final instructions to him were laced with double meaning, littered with innuendo, and from Dante's tense expression she knew he felt each one.

'No, Dante, *you* need to listen. This garden may look beautiful now, but tomorrow when I've cleaned up and gone, you'll come for another look and see its apparent faults. Tomorrow, in the cold light of day, you'll wonder what the hell you paid all this money for, because the lights won't be on and the bushes will look a bit smaller and sparser than they do tonight. You'll see all the lines where the turf was laid and the sticks holding up the plants and—'

'It will still be beautiful to me,' Dante interrupted. 'Because it's already given me more pleasure than I ever thought possible.' And, yes, he was talking about Alex, because his hands were gesturing to where his daughter sat, but his eyes were holding hers as he spoke and she knew that he was also referring to them. 'Yes, it might just take a bit of getting used to, but I can understand now that in the end it would be worth it…' She stared back at him for the longest time, swallowing hard as he went on. 'That if I nurture it, care for it, tend it…' With each word he tempted her, delivering his veiled apology in a low silken drawl. 'Then it will reward me tenfold.'

'It would have,' Matilda said softly, watching his wince of regret at her refusal to accept it, actually grateful when Katrina and Hugh ducked inside the emerald canopy and broke the painful moment, because whatever Dante was trying to say it was too little, too late—even a garden full of flowers wasn't going to fix this.

'Join us for a drink,' Hugh offered. 'Dante's just about to put Alex to bed…'

'I've got too much to do here.' Matilda smiled as she shook her head. 'But thank you for the offer.'

'I think we might have to stay over.' Katrina pretended to grimace. 'Hugh's had a couple too many champagnes to drive.'

'I've had one,' Hugh said, but Katrina had clearly already made up her mind. Matilda was tempted to tell her that she needn't bother, that Dante didn't need to be guarded on her final night here, but instead she offered her goodnights and headed to the mountain of tools that needed to be sorted.

'You really ought to think about finishing up,' Dante called. 'There's a storm brewing and with all these cables and everything it could be hazardous.'

She didn't even deign a response, grateful when they left, when finally the garden gate closed and she was alone.

* * *

Despite her utter exhaustion, working a sixteen-hour day, when finally Matilda showered and fell into bed, sleep evaded her, the body Dante had awoken then tossed aside twitching with treacherous desire. Lying in the darkness, she gazed out over the bay, watching the dark clouds gathering in the distance, the ominous view matching her mood as she listened to the talking and laughter coming from the garden below. Katrina's grating voice telling tales about the wonderful Jasmine did nothing to soothe her and she wished over and over that she'd managed to avoid Dante tonight.

Reluctantly she replayed his words in her mind. With total recall she remembered the look on his face as he had spoken to her, and she knew that she'd almost forgiven him, that had he touched her, she'd have gone to him.

A whimpering cry carried down the hallway and Matilda listened as Alex called out in her sleep. Her first instinct was to go to the little girl, but she stayed put, knowing that Dante would hear her on the intercom. She waited for the sound of his footsteps on the stairs, but they never came. Alex's cries grew louder and more anguished and Matilda screwed her eyes closed and covered her ears with her hands in an attempt to block them out, knowing that it was none of her business, while praying someone would come soon.

'Mama!'

Alex's terrified little voice had Matilda sitting bolt upright in bed, the jumbled babbles of a child's nightmare tearing at her heartstrings until she could bear it no more. The sensible thing would have been to go downstairs and alert Dante, and she had every intention of doing so, even pulling on a pair of knickers for manners' sake! But as she padded down the hallway in her flimsy, short nightdress, as the screams got louder, instinct kicked in, and pushing open the bedroom door, she called out to Alex in the darkness, gathering the hot, tear-racked body in her arms and attempting to soothe her, trying not to convey her alarm as Alex sobbed harder, her balled fists attempting to slam into Matilda's cheeks.

'Shush, honey,' Matilda soothed, capturing her wrists. Instead of holding her away, she brought a hand up to her face, controlling the movement, stroking her face with Alex's hand as over and over she told her that everything was OK, relief filling her as gradually the child seemed to calm.

'It's OK, Alex.' Over and over she said it, even letting go of Alex's wrist as finally the little girl started to relax, rocking her gently in her arms.

'What happened?'

She'd been so focused on Alex, Matilda hadn't even heard him come in, but as his deep-voiced whisper reached her ears, for Alex's sake she forced herself not to tense, just carried on rocking the child as she spoke.

'She was screaming. I was going to come and get you, but…' Her voice trailed off. How could she tell him that she'd been unable to just walk past? 'I thought you'd hear her on the intercom.'

'It's not working—there's a storm coming so it's picking up interference.' He was standing over her now and she assumed he'd take Alex from her, but she was wrong. Instead, he gazed down at his daughter, his hand stroking her forehead, pushing back the damp blonde curls from her hot, red face. 'She was really upset,' Dante observed, then looked over at Matilda. 'And you managed to calm her.'

'I just cuddled her,' Matilda said, 'as you do, and spoke to her.'

'No one can usually calm her.' Dante blinked. 'No one except me and sometimes Katrina.'

They stood in silence for the longest time, a deep, pensive silence broken only by the fading sobs of Alex, until finally she was quiet, finally she gave in. 'I think she's asleep,' Matilda whispered, gently placing Alex back in her cot, grateful she'd remembered to put on knickers as she lowered the little body.

'It's hot in here,' Date said, his voice not quite steady. As he opened the window a fraction more, the sweet scent of jasmine filled the air. Matilda stepped back as Dante took over tucking the sheets around Alex, tears filling her eyes as he placed a tender kiss on his daughter's cheek until she could bear it no more, the agony of witnessing such an intimate scene more than she could take. Matilda headed out into the hall, wiping the tears with the backs of her hands, cringing as his hand closed around her shoulder, as Dante tried to stop her.

'Matilda…'

'Don't,' Matilda begged, because she knew what was coming, knew he was going to apologise again, and she was terrified she'd relent. 'Just leave me alone, Dante.'

'I cannot do that.' His hand was still on her shoulder but she shook it off, turned her expressive face to his, the anger that had never really abated brimming over again. Aware of Alex, she struggled to keep her voice down.

'Why me?' she whispered angrily, tears spilling down her face as she glared at him. 'Why, when you could have any woman you wanted, did you have to pick on me?' Her hoarse whisper trailed off as she heard Hugh and Katrina at the foot of the stairs. Horrified, she stared at him, excruciatingly aware of her lack of attire, knowing how it would appear and not up to the confrontation.

His reflexes were like lightning. His hand closed around hers and in one movement he opened a door, practically pulling her inside, but she was plunged from desperation to hell. The mocking sight of his bedroom twisted the knife further, if that were possible, and she let him have it, her fists balling like Alex's, pushing against his chest as she choked the words out. 'You knew what this would do to me. You knew how much this would hurt me in the end. So why did you even start it, why, when you could have anyone, did you have to pick on me?'

'Shh,' Dante warned, the voices on the other side of the door growing nearer, but Matilda was past caring now.

'Why,' she said nastily, 'are you worried what Katrina will say?' She never got to finish. Both his hands were holding hers so he silenced her in the only way he could, his mouth pressing on hers, pushing her furious body against the door as she resisted with every fibre of her being, clamping her mouth closed, trying not to even breathe because she didn't want to taste him, smell him, didn't want to taste what she could never have again.

''Night, Dante…'

A million miles away on the other side of the door Katrina called to him. Warning her with his eyes, he moved his mouth away, his breath hot on her cheeks, his mouth ready to claim hers again if she made a single move.

''Night, Katrina.'

And shame licked the edges then, shame trickling in as he stared down at her till the moment had passed, till Hugh and Katrina were safely out of earshot and Dante told her a necessary home truth.

'I do not have to answer to Katrina, but I do respect her, Matilda. She is the mother of my wife and the grandmother of my child. I will not flaunt a relationship in front of her without fair warning.'

'What relationship?' Matilda sneered, but her face was scarlet, knowing that in this instance he was right. 'Sex with no strings isn't enough for me, Dante.' Which was such a contrary thing to say when her whole body was screaming for him, her nipples like stinging thistles against her nightdress, her body trembling with desire, awoken again by the one-sided kiss.

'It isn't enough for me either,' Dante said softly. 'At least not since you came along.' His hands had loosened their grip but his eyes were pinning her now, and she stared back, stunned, sure she must have somehow misheard. She dropped her eyes, didn't want to look at him when surely he would break her heart again, but his hand cupped her chin, capturing her, ensuring that she remained looking at him, his fingers softly holding her, his thumb catching tears as they tumbled down her cheeks. 'A lady who asks me for directions, a lady who steps into a elevator and into my life. It was I who wanted to see you again. Hugh told me to cancel that dinner, it was I was who insisted that we go ahead…' Utterly bemused, drenched in hope, she blinked back at him, struggled to focus as she shifted the murky kaleidoscope of the their brief past into glorious Technicolor. 'I had to kiss you. I convinced myself that when I did it would be over, but no…' It was Dante who appeared confused how, Dante shaking his head as he recalled. 'Like a drug, I need more, we make love and still I tell myself that it is just need that propels me, male needs, that when the garden is finished then so too will we be. I don't want to feel this, Matilda…'

'Why?' Matilda begged. 'Because of Jasmine?'

Pain flickered across his face and for a fragment of time she wished she could retract, take back what she had just said, yet somehow Matilda knew it had to be faced, that they could only glimpse the future if he let her into the past. But Dante shook his head, refuted her allegation almost instantly.

'Alex is the one who has to come first…'

'She will,' Matilda breathed, sure that wasn't the entire issue, sure that, despite his denial, and his apparent openness, still he was holding back. But as he pulled her into his arms, as he obliterated the world with his masterful touch, she let it go, reassured by his words and a glimpse of the future with Dante by her side and utterly sure she had all the time in the world to source his pain.

One hand was circling the back of her neck now, tiny circular motions that were incredibly soothing but at the same time incredibly erotic. She could feel the steady hammer of his heart against her ear, inhale the unique maleness of him as his gentle words reached her, his lips shivering along the hollow of her neck, moving down to the creamy flesh of her shoulder. His teeth nibbled at the spaghetti strap of her nightdress, his tongue cool against her burning skin, eyes closing as, giddy with want, he pulled the delicate garment downwards, sliding it over her breasts. His hands lingered over her hips as, guided by him, she stepped out of it, facing him now with a mixture of nervousness and raw sexuality, naked apart from the palest of pink silk panties. And the low moan of desire that escaped his lips erased for ever the poisonous roots of self-doubt Edward had so firmly planted, her body fizzing with new hope and desire as he sank to his knees, knowing that to Dante she was beautiful.

His hands were still on her hips but he was kissing her stomach now, deep, throaty kisses that were as faint-making as they were erotic. She could feel his tongue on her skin and it was overwhelming, her tummy tightening in reflex as one hand slipped between her thighs, stroking the pale, tender skin on the inside as his lips moved down. She could feel the heat through the cool silk fabric, his tongue, his lips on her making her weak with want, desperate for him to rip at her panties, to satisfy the desire that was raging in her. She gave tiny gasps in her throat as her fingers knotted together in his hair, as still he teased her more, his teeth grazing the silk, his tongue moistening her more, and even if it was everything she wanted, it still wasn't enough. Realisation hit her that, despite what had taken place in the garden, she'd never seen him naked. Need propelling her, she pulled back a touch, saw the question in his eyes as slowly he stood up. Her fingers, nervous at first, but bolder as desire took over, wrestled with the buttons of his shirt, pushing the sleeves down over his muscular arms. Closing her eyes in giddy want, her pale breasts pressed against his chest. She felt the naked silk of his dark skin against her, skin on skin, as she opened his belt and unzipped his shorts. She held her breath in wonder as Dante now shed the garments that stood between them, and if he'd been beautiful before, he was stunning now.

Never had she seen a more delicious man, his body toned and muscular, his dark, olive skin such a contrast to hers, the ebony of the hair that fanned on his chest tapering down into a delicious, snaky black line that led to the most decadent, delicious male centre. His arousal was terrifying and exciting at the same time, jutting out of silky black hair, proud and angry and alive, and the bed that had looked so daunting was just a tiny breathless step away. As they lay face to face she held him in her hand, marvelling at the strength, the satin softness of the skin that belied the steel beneath it, nervous, tentative at first. But his tiny moans of approval told her she was doing it right. Her other hand was audacious too, cupping his heavy scrotum, holding all of him, and loving it, as his lips found her breasts, suckling on her tender flesh, a tiny gasp catching in her throat as felt him growing stronger, nearer.

'Careful.' His voice was thick with lust as his hand captured her wrist, stopped her just in time, and she was greedy now for her turn, biting down on her bottom lip as he ran the tip of his erection over her panties, could see the tiny silver flash that told her he was near. She almost wept with voracious need as his finger slipped inside the fabric, gently parting her pink, intimate lips, sliding deep inside as still he teased her on the outside, sliding his heat against her till she was frenzied, her neck arching backwards, her whole body rigid, fizzing with want.

And Dante was the same, she knew it, as he tore at the delicate panties, ripped them open and plunged deep inside, her orgasm there to greet him, her intimate vise twitching around him as he entered, thrusting inside her. And yet he made her wait for his, their heated bodies moving together, long, delicious strokes as his moist skin slid over hers, her orgasm fading then rising again as he worked deliciously on, her fingers clutching his taut buttocks, her neck rigid as his tongue, his mouth devoured it, tasting her, relishing her, arousing her all over again. She could feel the tension in him building, his movements faster now, delicious involuntary thrusts as his body dictated the rhythm for both of them, no turning back as he drove them both forward.

He spilled inside her as she came again, crying out his name as he took her higher than she had ever been then held her as she came back down. But if making love with Dante had been exquisite, nothing could rival the feeling of him holding her in his arms, his body spooning into her warm back, the bliss of being held by him, his tender, warm hand on her stomach, his breathing evening out, experiencing the beauty of a bed shared tonight.

And the promise tomorrow could bring.

CHAPTER TEN

'DANTE!'

She barely said it, more breathed the word, her eyes snapping open as the bedroom door opened. A tiny rigid figure was silhouetted in the doorway, staring at the vast bed, and all Matilda knew was that Alex mustn't see her. She wriggled slightly in his arms, pulling her legs down straight, trying to remain inconspicuous yet somehow awaken him. Gently she prodded him, slipping beneath the covers as he came to, feeling like an intruder hiding, chewing on her bottom lip and cringing inside as Dante took in the scene.

'Alex, darling.' She could feel him pull back the covers, groping on the floor for his boxers then stepping out of the bed and crossing the room. 'Did something wake you?'

And because it was Alex, there was no answer to his question. Instead, Matilda listened to his comforting words as he scooped the little girl up and carried her back towards her bedroom. She waited till the coast was clear before wrapping the sheet around her and heading for the *en suite,* pulling on Dante's bathrobe and, despite the oppressive heat of the night, heading back to the bed to sit and shiver on the edge till Dante returned.

'Is she OK?' Worried eyes jerked to his. 'I don't think she saw me. It's so dark in here I'm sure that she couldn't have. I just heard the door open…'

'She's fine,' Dante instantly reassured her. 'I gave her a drink of water and she settled back down. I don't know what's wrong with her tonight…' Sitting down on the bed, he wrapped an arm around her, but she could sense his distraction, knew that he was worried about what Alex might have seen.

'I heard the door open and saw her. I honestly don't think that she saw me. The only reason I could make her out was because the hall light was on. As soon as I heard something, I slipped under the covers.'

'She didn't seem worried,' Dante agreed. 'I think she was just thirsty…' His voice trailed off and Matilda watched as he raked his fingers through his hair, seeing him now not as a lover but as the father he was…

Would always be.

'I'll go back to my room.'

'No.' He shook his head, one hand reaching out and attempting to grab her wrist. But Matilda captured it, holding his strong hand in her gentler one. And as much as she didn't want to go, as much as she knew Dante wanted her to stay, she knew it was right to leave.

'Dante, it's fine. Alex might come back and neither of us is going to relax now. I'll go and sleep in my room. It's better that way. We've got away with it once…'

'You understand?'

'Completely,' Matilda said softly, her free hand capturing his cheek, feeling the scratch of his stubble beneath her fingers. Although she longed to sleep with him, to wake up with him, she knew some things were more important, knew that she had to act unselfishly now. 'You need to be here for Alex,' she whispered, kissing his taut cheek, feeling the tension in his body as she held him for a precious second, knowing he was torn between want and duty, knowing that she could make things easier for him by going.

And it wasn't a small comfort as she slipped into her king-sized single bed, still wrapped in his robe, still warm from his touch, his intimate spill still moist between her legs. It was the most grown-up decision she'd ever made.

It was love.

'Dante!'

Brutally awoken by the piercing shout, Matilda sat up in bed, her mind whirling as chaos broke out. She tried to piece together the events of the night before and failed as the urgent events of today thundered in.

'Where is she?'

Wrapping the tie of Dante's bathrobe around her, Matilda climbed out of bed, her heart hammering at the urgency in Katrina's voice, waiting, *waiting* for Dante to reply. For him to tell her that Alex was in bed with him. Her stomach turned as she opened her bedroom door and saw Dante's pale, anguished face as he ran the length of the hallway, desperation in his voice as he called his daughter's name, terrified, frenzied eyes meeting hers as he explained the appalling situation.

'Alex isn't in her bed. We can't find her.'

Dashing down the hallway, she careered into Dante, his face a mixture of fixed determination and wretched pain.

'The pool!' They both said it at the same time. His worst nightmare eventuating, she followed him, bare feet barely touching the surface, jumping, running, taking the stairs two, three at a time as her mind reasoned. The pool was fenced and gated, Matilda attempted to reason as she ran; Dante was always so careful with his daughter's security there was no way Alex could have got in. As she dashed across the lawn, Dante was miles ahead, naked apart from his boxers, his whole body taut with dread. Finally she reached him, shared in that anguished look at the cool glittering blue surface. But there was little solace to be taken. The glimmering bay twinkled in the sunrise, a vast ocean just metres away and a tiny, fragile child missing.

'Call the police.' Dante's voice was calm but his lips were tight, a muscle hammering in his cheek as his idyllic, bayside view turned again to torture. 'Tell them to alert the coastguard.'

'She was fine last night!' Katrina's brittle voice grated on Matilda's already shot nerves. The police had long since arrived, their radios crackling in the background as officers started the appalling process—interviewing the adults, searching the house and gardens. A frantic race against time ensued. She could hear the whir of helicopter rotors as they swooped along the coastline. As she stared at Dante, who had returned at the police's bidding from a frantic race to the beach to look for his daughter, sand on his damp legs, his proud face utterly shattered, her first instinct was to reach out and hold him, to comfort him, but aware of Katrina and how it would look, she held back. 'I looked in on her as I went to bed…'

'What time was that?' An incredibly young officer asked as another sat writing notes.

'Eleven, twelve perhaps,' Katrina responded. 'Dante had already gone up.'

'So you were the last person to see her?'

'No,' Dante broke in. 'I was the last person to see her.' Matilda held her breath as he carried on talking, wondering if he would reveal what had happened and with a sinking heart knowing that he had to. 'She was distressed when I went up, but she went back to sleep. Katrina would have seen her a few moment after that, but a couple of hours later she came into my room.'

'She'd climbed out of her cot?'

'She's started to do that,' Dante said, raking his fingers through his hair, his whole body in abject pain. She ached to comfort him yet sat completely still as he spoke on. 'She seemed thirsty so I gave her a drink and cuddled her for a moment.'

'Was she upset?'

'No.' Dante shook his head, his face contorting with agonized concentration as he recalled every detail of the last time he had seen his daughter. 'At least, I don't think so.'

'You don't think so?' the policeman pushed, and Matilda could have slapped him for his insensitivity. But Dante was calmer, explaining Alex's problem in a measured voice, but his voice was loaded with pain.

'My daughter has problems—behavioural problems.' Katrina opened her mouth to argue, but Dante stood firm, shaking his head at Katrina, clearly indicating that now wasn't the time for futile denial. 'She doesn't react in the usual way—you never really know what she's thinking. Look, you *have* to tell your colleagues that they could be just a metre away from her, could be calling her name, and she won't answer them, she won't call out…' His voice broke for a second and Matilda watched as he attempted to recover, his eyes closing for an agonising second as he forced himself to continue. 'You have to tell them that.'

The officer nodded to his partner, who left the room to impart the news before he continued with the interview. 'You gave her a drink—then what?'

'I opened the window a fraction more—there are locks on it, so she could never have opened it wide enough to get out. Her room was…' His English momentarily failed him. Dante balled his fists in frustration as he tried to give the police officer each and every piece of information he could. 'Confined,' he attempted. 'With the storm coming and everything…' As if in answer, a crack of thunder sounded and Matilda watched the fear dart in his eyes. The rain started to pelt on the window, each drop ramming home the fact that his baby was out there with the elements

'Anything else?' the officer checked. 'Is there anything else that happened last night that was out of the ordinary? Any strange sounds, phone calls—anything, no matter how irrelevant it might seem, that might have upset your daughter?'

Dante's eyes met Matilda's.

'No.' He shook his head, dragged his eyes away but his expression haunted her. The guilt in his eyes as he bypassed the truth made her know without hesitation what was coming next, that the only person Dante wanted to protect here, and rightly so, was his daughter.

'Officer, may I speak to you outside?'

'About what?' Katrina demanded as the two of them walked out of the room. 'What aren't you telling us, Dante? What happened last night that you can't say in front of me?'

Embarrassed, terrified, Matilda stood there as Katrina answered her own question.

'You tart,' Katrina snarled, and Matilda winced at the venom behind it. 'That's Dante's gown that you're wearing.' Katrina eyed Matilda with utter contempt but didn't leave it there. Her lips were white and rigid with hatred. 'You were in bed with Dante, weren't you? That's why the poor little mite ran off into the night!'

'I truly don't think that she saw me,' Matilda said. 'We were both asleep and she just pushed open the door…'

'And saw a woman who wasn't her mother in her father's bed! Do you realise what you have done, Matilda?' Disgust and fury were etched on Katrina's features and for an appalling moment Matilda thought that Katrina might even hit her. 'Do you have any idea the damage that you've done to my grandchild?'

'Leave it, Katrina.' Dante's voice was weary as he came back into the room, but it had a warning note to it that Katrina failed to heed.

'I most certainly will not leave it.' Furious eyes

swivelled between Dante and Matilda, her face contorted with disgust. 'Did Alex see you?' Her eyes were bulging in her head. 'That little girl walked in and found the pair of you—'

'It wasn't like that,' Matilda said, but Katrina shot her down in a second.

'Shut up!' she screamed. 'Shut the hell up. You have no say here! None at all.'

'Katrina.' Dante crossed the room, his face grey. 'This isn't helping…'

'Of course it isn't helping. How, Dante, did you think sleeping with her was going to help your daughter? How did you think shaming my daughter's memory like that was going to help Alex? But, then, I suppose you didn't even stop to think. I warned you, Dante, warned you to be careful, to keep things well away from Alex, and then some little—'

'I said leave it!' Still he didn't shout, but there was such icy power behind his words that even in full, rage-fuelled flood Katrina's voice trailed off. It was Matilda who stepped in. Running a dry tongue over her lips, she again attempted to calm things down.

'All we can do for now is give the police all the information we have and then look for Alex. Arguing isn't going to help.'

'She's right,' Dante said, addressing Katrina, which momentarily Matilda found strange. But she didn't hold the thought. Her mind was already racing ahead, trying to work out how they could find Alex, where the little girl might be. But as Dante continued talking, Matilda knew that the agony that had pierced her consciousness since awakening had only just begun, because nothing Katrina had said in rage could have hurt her more than the expression on Dante's face as he turned and finally faced her, his expression cold and closed, his eyes not even meeting hers.

'I think you should leave, Matilda…'

'Leave?' She shook her head, her voice incredulous, horrified by what he was saying. 'Don't shut me out now, Dante. Last night you said—'

'Last night you were his whore,' Katrina shouted. 'Last night he said what he had to, to get you to share his bed. Dante loved my daughter.' She was screeching now, almost deranged. 'Jasmine's barely cold in her grave. Did you really think you could fill her space? Did you really think he meant what he said, that he'd besmirch her memory with you?'

'No one's trying to besmirch Jasmine's memory,' Dante said, his face as white as marble as he turned to Katrina.

'No one could!' Katrina yelled. 'Because if you truly loved my daughter then last night can be nothing more than a fling and I know that you loved her. I know that!'

'I did.' Dante halted her tirade. 'I do,' he insisted, his hands spreading in the air in a helpless gesture, utter panic on his face as reality started to sink in. 'But right now all I can think of is Alex. All I know is that my baby is out there…'

'Let me help with the search,' Matilda pleaded, but Dante's back was to her, demanding action from the officer that stood there, picking up the phone and punching in numbers. 'Dante, please…'

'You want to help?' His face was unrecognisable as he finally faced her. 'If you really want to help, Matilda, you will do as I ask and just go home. It will be better.'

'Better for who?' Matilda whispered through chattering teeth, knowing the answer even before it came.

'Better for everyone.'

It took about ten minutes to pack, ten minutes to throw her things into her suitcase and drag it down the stairs, ten minutes to remove herself from Dante's life. The scream inside was a mere breath away, her teeth grinding together with the agony of keeping it all in. She wanted to slap him, to yell at him, confront him, couldn't believe that he'd done it to her again, that she'd been stupid enough to let him fool her, to be beguiled by him over again, but somehow she choked it down, the horror of a child missing overriding everything. She placed her own pain, her utter humiliation on total hold. Wincing against the sting of the rain on her bare arms, she threw her case into the boot, imagining its impact on a little girl dressed in nothing but pyjamas.

'We need a contact number, miss.' The young officer tapped on the steamed-up car window as Matilda started the engine. She scribbled her number on a piece of paper and handed it to him. 'Can I help—with the search I mean?'

'Hold on a second, love.' The policeman halted her as his radio crackled into life and Matilda waited, her heart in her mouth at the urgent note in the officer's voice, flashes of conversation reaching her ears.

'They've found her?' Matilda begged.

'I need to tell the child's father first.' He was making

to go but Matilda shot out of the car and ran alongside him as he headed for the house.

'How is she?' Matilda demanded. 'Is she okay?'

'I'm not sure,' the officer reluctantly answered. 'They found her wandering in some dunes. She seems OK but she's not talking. They're taking her to the local hospital…'

'She rarely speaks.' Matilda could feel relief literally flooding her at the seemingly good news. 'Oh, I have to tell Dante…'

'Miss I really think…' Something in his voice stilled her and, despite the police officer's youthful looks, Matilda saw the wisdom in his eyes as he offered some worldly advice for free. 'I think that for now at least you need to leave this family alone. Emotions are already pretty high. Give it a day or two and it will calm down, but I think the best thing you can do now is take Mr Costello's advice and go home.'

CHAPTER ELEVEN

EVERYTHING was hard—even tidying her tiny apartment required a mammoth effort, yet she felt compelled to do it. Despite her fatigue, and utter exhaustion, she needed to somehow clear the decks, to get things in order before she took on the even bigger task of getting on with the rest of her life.

A life without Dante.

Pushing the vacuum around, Matilda wished the noise from the machine could drown out her thoughts, wished she could just switch off her mind, find some peace from the endless conundrums.

Two weeks ago she hadn't even known he'd existed, he hadn't factored into even one facet of her life, and now he consumed her all—every pore, every breath every cell of her. She was drenched with him, possessed by him, yearned for him, but was furious with him, too. A molten river of anger bubbled over the edge of her grief every now and then that Dante would have let her leave without even knowing whether his daughter was alive or dead, assuming that the world ran on the same emotionless clock as he did, where feelings could be turned off like a light switch and the truth distorted enough to conjure up reasonable doubt.

She'd been home four days now. Four days when he hadn't even bothered to pick up the phone and let her know about Alex—surly she deserved that much at least?

For the first couple of nights Matilda had watched him on the nightly TV news, striding out of the court-room without comment. She had scanned the newspa-pers by day for a glimpse of him, trying to read mes-sages that weren't there in the tiny stilted statements that were quoted. But it had become unbearable, seeing him, reading about him yet knowing she couldn't have him, so instead she'd immersed herself in anything she could think of, anything that might turn her mind away from him and give her peace even for a moment. She knew it was useless, knew that she could work till she dropped, could fill her diary with engagements, could go out with friends every night, but she'd never fully escape, that all she could hope was that the agony might abate, might relent just enough to allow her to breathe a little more easily.

Kicking off the vacuum, Matilda gave in and padded towards the wardrobe, as she had done repeatedly for the last four days. She pulled out Dante's dressing-gown, which in her haste she had inadvertently packed, feeling the heavy fabric between her fingers, knowing that the sensible thing to do would be to throw it into the washing machine, to parcel it up and mail it to him. But it was the one task she was putting off, pathetically aware that apart from her bittersweet memories it was the only reminder of Dante she had. Sitting on the edge of the bed, she buried her face in the robe, dragging in his evocative aroma. And it was like feeling it all over again, every breath reinforcing the agony of his rejection, the blistering pain of his denial. A scent that had once been so beautiful was tainted now for ever. In fact, it almost made her feel nauseous now as she revisited the pain, the devastation…

'Alex!'

For the first time in days, Dante left her mind, the name of his daughter shivering out of her lips, but it wasn't a sob. Her tears turned off like a tap, thoughts, impossible, incredulous thoughts pinging in, realisation dawning. She shook her head to clear it, because surely it couldn't be so…surely the thought that had just occurred would be flawed on examination, that Alex's problems couldn't really be that simple. But instead, the more she thought about it the more sense it made, the more she had to share it.

'Hugh.' Her hands were shaking so much after several fruitless attempts to reach Dante that she'd had to dial his number several times. 'I need to speak to Dante. His phone's turned off, but is there any way when the court takes a break—'

'He's not here.' Hugh's voice was so flat, so low, that Matilda had to strain to catch it.

'Can you give me his secretary's number?' Matilda asked, shame and embarrassment pushed aside. Right now she didn't care about Dante's response to her—this was way, way more important.

'Matilda, have you seen the newspaper, the television?' Hugh asked, as her free hand flicked on the remote, wondering what on earth Hugh was going on about. 'The charges were all dropped, the trial finished two days ago…'

'Two days ago?' Matilda's mind raced for comfort but there was none to be had. She couldn't even pretend it was because of the trial, because of work that he hadn't called her. But she dragged herself to the present, forced herself to focus on the reason she needed to talk to him so badly. 'Hugh, I need to speak to him urgently.' Her voice was the most assertive she'd ever heard it. 'Now, can you, please, tell me how I can get hold of him?'

'He's in Italy.' And even though she wanted to have misheard, even though at the eleventh hour she mentally begged for a reprieve, Matilda knew from the utter devastation in Hugh's voice that there wouldn't be one.

Dante really had gone.

'He's asked me not to ring for a few weeks, Matilda. He wants some time to sort things out and I've tried to respect that—not that it matters. I know that his housekeeper won't put me through and I'm pretty sure she wouldn't put…'

He didn't say it, didn't twist the taut knife any further, but they both knew the words that filled the silence that crackled down the telephone line. If he wouldn't even speak to Hugh, what hope was there of Dante speaking to her?

'Hugh.' Matilda's mind was going at a thousand miles an hour. She knew she couldn't tell Hugh what she thought she knew, couldn't build him up just to tear him down, knew she had to tread carefully now. 'Could I ask you to give me his address?'

'I don't know.' She could feel his hesitation, knew that she was asking him to cross a line, but she also knew that Hugh wanted Dante back in Australia more than anything in the world, and if something Matilda said could make that happen then perhaps it was worth a try. 'I guess it wouldn't do any harm to write to him, then it's up to Dante whether or not he reads it.'

Matilda held her breath as she scrabbled for a pen, then closed her eyes in blessed relief as finally, after the longest time, Hugh gave it to her.

'Thanks, Hugh.' Matilda said, clicking off the telephone, and even though it was the biggest, possibly the most reckless decision of her life, amazingly she didn't hesitate. She flicked through the phone book before making her second call of the day, knowing that if she thought about it, tried to rationalise it, she'd never do it.

'I'd like to book a flight to Rome, please.'

'When did you want to go?' Running a shaking hand through her hair, Matilda listened to the efficient voice, could hear the taps on the keyboard as the woman typed in the information. Taking a deep breath, she uttered the most terrifying words of her life.

'I'd like the next available flight, please.'

CHAPTER TWELVE

'I'M SORRY the flight has been overbooked.'

Matilda could barely take it in, just blinked back as the well-groomed woman tapped over and over at her computer. She was scarcely able to believe what she was hearing, that the seat she'd booked and paid for just a few short hours ago had never been available in the first place, that flights were often overbooked and that if she read the fine print on her ticket she'd realise that there was nothing she could do—that she'd just have to wait until the next flight.

'When is the next flight?' Matilda's trembling voice asked, watching the long, immaculately polished nails stroking the keyboards.

'I can get you on tomorrow at eleven a.m.'

She might just as well have said the next millennium, Matilda realised, because her conviction left her then, the conviction that had forced her to pick up the telephone and book her flight, the conviction that had seen her pack at lightning speed, cancel work, persuade her family, hissed out of her like the air in a balloon when the party was over. And it *was* over, Matilda realised.

If ever she'd wanted a sign, this was it—and it wasn't a subtle one. Neon lights flashing over the ground steward's head couldn't have spelt it out clearer.

She'd been stupid to think she could do it, could convince Dante what she felt in her heart was wrong with Alex. Her family, her friends had all poured scorn on the idea, even she herself had when she'd attempted to write down what was screaming so clearly in her mind. That was the reason she had to see Dante face to face, *had* to tell him now, couldn't put it in a letter, couldn't wait for tomorrow, because only now could she really believe it—only now, before her argument was swayed, before she attempted to rationalise what she was sure was true.

Was true because she'd felt it herself.

Had felt it.

'We can offer a refund.'

'I don't want a refund.' Matilda shook her head. 'I have to get this flight.' She heard the words, knew it was her own voice, but even she couldn't believe the strength behind it. 'I have to get this flight because if I don't get on this plane tonight, I know that I'm never going to…'

And she'd watched the airport shows, had watched passengers pleading their cases, shouting their rage, and had winced from the comfort of her sofa, knowing that no matter how loud they shouted, if the flight was full, if the gate was closed, then they might as well just give up now.

'Gate 10.'

'Sorry?' Matilda started, watching as a tag was swiftly

clipped around a rather shabby suitcase before it bumped out of view, watching as those manicured fingers caught the boarding pass from the printer and offered it to her.

'Gate 10,' came the clipped voice. 'Business and first class are boarding now—you'd better step on it.'

And the most infrequent of frequent flyers Matilda might have been, but she wasn't a complete novice either. Her overwrought mind worked overtime as she made it through passport control then dashed along the carpeted floors of Melbourne airport, walked along the long passageway, knowing that the comfort level of the next twenty-four hours was entirely dependent on a single gesture.

Right for Economy.

Left for Business.

'Good evening, Miss Hamilton.' Blond, gorgeous and delightfully gay, the flight attendant greeted her and Matilda held her breath, playing a perverse game of he loves me, he loves me not. He checked her ticket and gestured her to her seat.

'Straight through to your left, first row behind the curtain.'

And it didn't matter if he loved her or he loved her not, Matilda decided, slipping into her huge seat and declining an orange juice but accepting champagne in a glass. It didn't matter that she couldn't really afford the air fare and that if she lived to be a thousand she'd never be able to justify flying to the other side of the world on a hunch. If she'd wanted a sign then she had one. She really was doing the right thing, not for herself, not even for Dante…but for Alex.

* * *

Rome, Matilda decided, had to be the most beautiful city in the world, because jet-lagged, at six a.m. on a cold grey morning and nursing a broken heart, nothing in the world should have been able to lift her spirits, but hurtling through the streets of the Eternal City in a taxi, Matilda was captivated. So captivated that when the hotel receptionist informed her in no uncertain terms that her room wouldn't be ready for a couple more hours, Matilda was happy to leave her rather small suitcase at the hotel and wander the streets, plunged from the boskiness of a late Australian spring to a crisp Italian autumn.

A fascinated bystander, Matilda watched as the Eternal City awoke, the roads noisily filling up, cars, scooters, cycles, the pavements spilling over with beautiful, elegant people, chattering loudly in their lyrical language as they raced confidently past or halted a moment for an impossibly strong coffee. Everyone, except for her, seemed to know their place, know where they were going. Matilda, in contrast, meandered along cobbled streets which were rich with history, yet welcomed the modern—buildings that had stood for centuries housing a treasure trove of modern fashion, glimpsing a part of Dante's world and knowing that he was near. Wondering how to face him, how to approach him, how to let him know that she was there.

Message Sent

Matilda stared at the screen of her much-hated phone and for the first time was actually grateful to have it. Grateful for the ease of rapid contact without speech.

Well, not that rapid, Matilda thought ordering another latté to replace her long since cold one, watching as some fabulous, twenty-first-century Sophia Loren managed to drink, smoke, read and text at the same time. After a few failed attempts she'd managed to get her message across, had told Dante where she was now and where she would be staying later and asking if they could meet for a discussion—snappy, direct and impersonal.

Everything she'd tried and failed to be.

But when her message brought no response, when, looking at her watch, Matilda realised her room would be ready and she pulled out her purse and unpeeled the unfamiliar money, only then did the magnitude of what she had done actually catch up with her. Nerves truly hit as she realised that for all she knew, Dante might not even be in Italy—he could have stopped in Bangkok or Singapore for a break. It had seemed so important to see him at the time, it had never actually dawned on her that Dante might not want to see her, that she could have come all this way only to find out that he didn't even care what she had to say. Maybe she should have made it clear that she'd come to talk about Alex. Perhaps if she texted him again…

'Matilda.'

Thankful that her fingers were still in her purse and not creeping towards her phone, Matilda took the longest time to look up—truly unsure how she felt when she finally stared into the face whose loss she had been mourning. He looked older somehow, his skin a touch paler, the shadows under his eyes like bruises now, as if all the trouble of the past eighteen months had finally caught up with him—nothing like the dashing young barrister who'd walked out of a Melbourne courtroom a few days ago. Clearly he hadn't shaved since then, but instead of looking scruffy it gave him a slightly tortured, artistic look. Matilda decided, as he slid into the seat next to her and consumed her all over again, there was still more than a dash of the old Dante, still that irrefutable sex appeal.

Odd that when there was so much to say, when it was so outlandish that she was actually here, that the silence they sat in for a few moments wasn't particularly uncomfortable. Matilda gathered the images that fluttered in her mind, knowing she would take them out and explore them later. Dante accepted the coffee and plate of *biscotti* from the waiter and pushed them towards her.

'No, thanks.' Matilda shook her head and Dante obviously wasn't hungry either because he pushed the plate away untouched.

'Seems I was wrong about you,' he said finally. 'You're not afraid of confrontation after all.'

'Actually, you were right.' Matilda gave a pale smile. 'I'm not here to confront you, Dante.' She watched as his eyes narrowed. 'Whatever your opinion of me, please, know that I've got a better one of myself, and chasing after a man who clearly doesn't want me has never been my style.'

She watched his face harden, watched his jaw crease as if swallowing some vile taste down before speaking, his voice almost derisive because clearly he thought he knew better than her, clearly he assumed that she was lying. 'So why are you here, then, Matilda? If not about us, why are you here in Rome?'

'I'm here about Alex.' It was obviously the last thing he'd expected her to say because his face flickered in confusion, his eyes frowning as she continued. 'I think I know what's wrong with her. I think I've worked out what causes her to get upset, why she continues…'

'Matilda.' In a supremely Latin gesture he flicked her words away with his hands. 'I have consulted with the top specialists, I have had my daughter examined from head to toe and you, after one week of knowing her, after barely spending—'

'It's jasmine.' The two words stopped him in mid-sentence. His mouth opened to continue, to no doubt tell her she had no idea what she was talking about, but her urgent voice overrode him, her frantic eyes pinning him. Matilda knew if he would only listen to her for a single minute then it had to be a valuable one, that even if he didn't believe her now then maybe tonight, next week, next month, when they were both out of each other's lives for ever, when the pain of this moment had passed, he would recall her words objectively and maybe, maybe they'd make sense.

'The *scent* of jasmine,' Matilda specified, as Dante shook his head. 'That first day she lost her temper, the first day you called for a doctor, you told me you were on your way to the cemetery.'

'So?'

'Did you take flowers?' When he didn't respond she pushed harder, her heart hammering in her chest, because if she'd got this bit mistaken then her whole theory fell apart. But as she spoke Dante blinked a couple of times, his scathing face swinging around in alarm as she asked her next question. 'Did you take some jasmine from the garden?'

'Of course. But—'

'You sent flowers the day Jasmine died, Dante,' she said softly. 'And Katrina told me you'd had every florist in Melbourne trying to find some jasmine. Alex was trapped in a car for two hours with her mother, calling out for her, desperate for reassurance, trapped with that smell…'

'But a scent cannot trigger such a reaction.' Dante shook his head in firm denial, absolutely refusing to believe it could be so simple. But at least he was listening, Matilda consoled herself as she carried on talking, her own conviction growing with each word she uttered, the hunch that had brought her to this point a matter of fact now.

'Alex's trouble started in spring, Dante, when the jasmine was flowering, and when it became too much, when all she got was worse, you took her back to Italy…'

'Things were better for a while,' Dante argued. 'She was fine until…' His hand was over his mouth, his eyes widening as Matilda said it for him.

'Until spring came again. Dante, she didn't run away because she saw us in bed. Alex ran away because you opened the window. It was humid, the scent would have filled the room…'

'She was trying to get away from it?'

'I don't know,' Matilda whispered. 'I don't know what she's thinking. I just know that I'm right, Dante.'

'Suppose that you are.' His eyes were almost defiant.

'What am I supposed to do? I can hardly rid the world of jasmine, ensure she never inhales that scent again…'

'Why do you always have to go to such extremes, Dante? Why does it always have to be black and white to you? Oh, this isn't working so I'll leave the country. She seems nice, so I'll just be mean. Alex reacts to jasmine, so I'd better get rid of it. Just acknowledge it, Dante, and then find out how to work through it. Tell the experts, the doctors…' She gave a helpless shrug, then picked up her purse and put it firmly in her bag—hell, he could buy her a coffee at least.

'You're going?' Dante frowned as she stood.

'That's all I came here to say.'

'That's all?' Dante scorned, clearly not believing a word. 'You could have put that in a letter, rung me.'

'Would you have read it?' Matilda checked. 'Would you have picked up the phone? And even if you had, would you really have believed it without seeing me?'

'Probably not,' Dante admitted.

'Well, there you go,' Matilda said, heading for the door and out into the cool morning. She stilled as he called out to her, his skeptical voice reaching her ears.

'You're asking me to believe you flew to the other side of the world for a child you have seen four maybe five times.'

'I'm not *asking* you to believe anything, Dante.' The lid was off now, rivers of lava spewing over the edges as she turned round and walked smartly back to where he was standing, her pale face livid as she looked angrily up to him. 'I'm *telling* you that I didn't come here to discuss us. Get it into your head, I don't need a grand closing speech from you, there's no jury you have to sum up for here. You walked out without so much as a goodbye and that's a clear enough message even for me. I'm certainly not going to hover on the edges of your emotions, either waiting for permission to enter or to be told again to leave.'

'I told you from the start that there could be no relationship,' Dante said through gritted teeth.

'Well, you were right.' Matilda nodded. 'Because a relationship is about trusting and sharing and giving, and you're incapable of all three.'

'Matilda, I have a child who is sick and getting worse by the day. I was doing you a favour by holding back. How could I ask you to turn your life around for us? It's better this way…'

'Don't you dare!' Matilda roared, startling Dante and everyone in earshot. Even if the Italians were used to uncensored passion, clearly eight-thirty on a weekday morning was a little early for them. But Matilda was operating on a different time clock. It was the middle of the night in her mind as her emotions finally erupted, oblivious of the gathering crowd as finally she let him have it. 'Don't you dare decide what's best for me when you didn't even have the manners to ask. I loved you and you didn't want it. Well, fine, walk away, get on a plane and leave the country, walk out of my life without a goodbye, but don't you dare tell me it's for the best, don't you dare stand there and tell me that you're doing me a favour—when I never asked for one. I flew to the other side of the world because I care about your daughter and in time I'd have loved Alex, too. I'd have loved Alex because she was a part of you, and you *know* that, you *know* that, Dante.' She jabbed a finger into his chest, jabbed the words at him over and over, ramming the truth home to the motionless, rigid man. 'You didn't want my love—that's the bottom line so don't dress it up with excuses. You love Jasmine and you always will.'

'I loved Jasmine—' He started but she turned to walk away because she couldn't bear to look at him. She pushed her way through the little gathered crowd and started to run because she couldn't bear to be close to him and not have him, couldn't be strong for even a second longer. She'd said all she had come to and way, way more, had told him her truth. There was nothing left to give and certainly nothing more to take. She didn't want his crumbs of comfort, didn't want to hear how in another place, another time, maybe they could have made it.

'Matilda.' He caught her wrist but she couldn't take the contact, the shooting awareness that had propelled them on that first day even more acute, even more torturous. She tried to wrench it away, but he gripped it tighter, forced her to turn around and face him. '*Senti,*' he demanded. 'Listen to me!' But she shook her head.

'No, because there's nothing else to say.'

'Please?'

That one word stilled her, the one word she'd never heard him say, because he'd never had to ask politely for anything. Dante had never had to ask anyone for anything because it had all been there for the taking.

Till now.

'Please,' he said again, and she nodded tentatively. She felt his fingers loosen a touch round her wrist, grateful now for the contact as he led her away from the crowded streets and to the Villa Borghese, a green haven in the middle of the city. He led her through the park to a bench where they sat. Silent tears streaming down her face from her outpouring of emotion, she braced herself for the next onslaught of pain, biting on her lip as Dante implored her to listen, no doubt to tell her as he had in the first place why it could never, ever have worked.

'I loved Jasmine…' he said slowly, letting his hands warm hers. She was touching him for the last time, staring down at his long, manicured fingers entwined in hers and even managing a wan smile at the contrast, her hands certainly not her best feature. But it wasn't her short nails or her prolonged misuse of moisturiser that had Matilda frowning. Eyes that were swimming with tears struggled to focus on a gold band that was missing, a wedding band that to this day had always been there. Her confusion grew as Dante continued talking. 'But not like this.'

'Like what?' Matilda croaked, still staring at his naked ring finger.

'Like *this*.' Dante's voice was a hoarse whisper, but she could hear the passion and emotion behind it and something else that drew her eyes to his, recognition greeting her as Dante continued. '*This* love.'

He didn't have to elaborate because she knew exactly what he meant—*this* love that was all-consuming, *this* love that was so overwhelming and intense it could surely only be experienced once in a lifetime. And she glimpsed his hellish guilt then, guessed a little of what was coming next as he pulled her into his arms as if he needed to feel her to go on.

'We were arguing the day she died—we were always arguing.' He paused but she didn't fill it, knew Dante had to tell her his story himself. 'When I met Jasmine she was a career-woman and had absolutely no intention of settling down or starting a family, and that suited me fine. We were good together. I didn't have to explain the hours I put into my work and neither did she. It worked, Matilda, it really worked, until…' She felt him stiffen in her arms, felt him falter and held him just a touch tighter. 'Jasmine found out she was pregnant. We were both stunned. We'd taken precautions, it just wasn't part of the plan, wasn't what either of us wanted, and yet…' He pulled her chin up and she stared up at him, stared as that pain-ravaged face broke into a ghost of smile. 'I was pleased, too, excited. I loved her and she was having my baby, and I thought that would be enough.'

'But it wasn't?' Her voice was muffled by his embrace but Matilda already knew the answer.

'No.'

Or part of it.

'It wasn't enough for Jasmine. We got married quickly and bought this house and for a few months things were OK, but as Jasmine got bigger as the birth came closer, she seemed to resent the impact her pregnancy was having on her career. She was determined to go straight back to work afterwards, to carry on as if nothing had happened, and that is when the arguments started, because our baby was coming, like it or not, and things had to change. I tried to stay quiet, hoped that once the baby came she'd see things differently, but she didn't. She hired a top nanny and was back at work within six weeks, full time. She hardly saw Alex. I understand women work, I understand that, but not to the exclusion of their child, not when you don't need the money. That is when the arguments escalated.'

'People argue Dante…' Matilda tried to comfort him, tried to say the right thing, but knew it was useless. Despite their closeness, she could feel the wall around him, knew the pain behind it and ached to reach him, *ached* for him.

'She felt trapped, I know that,' Dante said, his voice utterly bleak. 'I know that, because so did I. Not that we ever said it, not that either of us had the courage to admit it. The morning of the accident, *again* she was going into the office. It was a Saturday and the nanny was off and *again* she wanted me to have Alex, only this time I said no. No. No. No…' He repeated the word like a torturous mantra. 'No. You are her mother. No, for once you have her. No, I'm going out. I told her it was wrong, that Alex deserved a better mother. I told her so many things terrible things…' She heard the break in his voice and moved to help him.

'Dante, people say terrible things in an argument. You just didn't get the chance to take them back.'

'I tried to—even as I was saying them I wanted it to stop, to put the genie back in the bottle and retract the things I had said. I did not want it to be over, I did not want Alex to come from a broken home. I rang the housekeeper and was told Jasmine had taken Alex to work with her. She wouldn't pick up when I called and I had the florist send flowers over to her office. I told them to write that all I wanted was for her to come home… She never did.'

'Oh, God, Dante…' Matilda knew she was supposed to be strong now, to somehow magic up the right words, but all she could do was cry—for him, for Jasmine and for the stupid mess that was no one's fault, for the pain, for both of them.

'She *was* coming home, Dante,' Matilda said finally, pressing her cheek against his, trying to instil warmth where there was none, her tears mingling with his. 'She got the flowers, she knew you were sorry…'

'Not sorry enough, though.' He closed his eyes in bitter regret, self-loathing distorting his beautiful features. 'Not sorry enough, because I was still angry. The problems were all still there and even if she hadn't died, I know deep down that sooner or later our marriage would have.'

'You don't know that, Dante, because you never got the chance to find out,' Matilda said softly. 'Who knows what would have happened if Jasmine had come home that day? Maybe you would have talked, would have sorted things out…'

'Maybe…' Dante said, but she could tell he didn't believe it, tell that he'd tried and failed to convince himself of the same thing. 'You know what I hate the most? I hate the sympathy, I hate that people think I deserve it.'

'You do deserve it,' Matilda said. 'Just because the two of you were having troubles, it doesn't mean you were bad people.'

'Perhaps,' Dante sighed. 'But I cannot burst Katrina and Hugh's bubble, cannot tell them that their daughter's last months were not happy ones…'

'You don't have to tell them anything.' Matilda shook her head. 'Tell them if you must that Jasmine made you so happy you want to do it all over again.' She cupped his proud face in her hand and forced him to look at her, smiled, not because it was funny but because it was so incredibly easy to help him, so incredibly *right* to lead him away from his pain. 'You did nothing wrong.

'*Nothing*,' she reiterated.

'But suppose that you'd walked into that lift two years ago, Matilda?' Dante asked. 'Suppose, after yet another row, the love of my life had appeared then? I punish Edward for what he did to you and yet…'

'Never.' Matilda shook her head, blew away his self-doubt with her utter conviction. 'You'd never have done that to Jasmine and you know that as much as I do, Dante, because even if the feelings had been there, you'd never have acted on them. My God, you're barely acting on them now, so surely you know that much about yourself.'

And he must have, because finally he nodded.

'Don't beat yourself up with questions you can never answer,' Matilda said softly. 'You and Jasmine did your best—just hold onto the fact that there was enough love to stop either of you walking away. You sent her flowers and asked her to come home and that's exactly what she was doing. The truth is enough to hold onto.'

And she watched as the pain that had been there since she'd first met him literally melted away, dark, troubled eyes glimmering with new-found hope. But it faded into a frown as Matilda's voice suddenly changed from understanding to angry, pulling back her hands and folding her arms, resting her chin on her chest and staring fixedly ahead. 'You're so bloody arrogant, Dante!'

'What the hell did I do now?' Dante asked, stunned at the sudden change in her.

'Sitting there and wondering whether or not you'd have had an affair with me! As if I had absolutely no say in the matter! Well, for your information, Dante Costello, I'd have slapped your damned cheek if you'd so much as laid a finger on me. I'd never get involved with a married man!'

'Unless he was your husband!' Dante said, uncoiling her rigid arms, kissing her face all over in such a heavenly Italian way. 'That was actually a proposal—just in case you were wondering.'

Matilda kissed him back with such passion and depth that if they had been in any city other than Rome, they'd no doubt have been arrested. It was Dante who pulled away, demanding a response from a grumbling Matilda, who wanted his kiss to go on for ever.

'That was actually a yes.' Matilda smiled, happy to go back to being ravished, to being kissed by the most difficult, complicated, beautiful man in the world. 'Just in case you were wondering!'

EPILOGUE

'ARE you OK?'

Standing in the garden—in *Alex's* garden—Matilda hastily wiped the tears from her cheeks as Dante approached, determined that he wouldn't see her cry. Today was surely hard enough for him without her tears making things worse.

'I'm fine,' Matilda answered, forcing a bright smile as she turned around. But watching him walk over, Alex running alongside him, Dante's hand shielding their newborn son's tiny face from the early morning sun with such tenderness, her reserve melted, the tears resuming as he joined her.

'It's OK to be sad,' Dante said softly. 'And you can't argue, because you said it yourself.'

'I did,' Matilda gulped, but as the sound of the removal trucks pulling into the drive reached her, she gave in, letting him hold her as she wept. 'I feel guilty for being upset at leaving when I know how much harder this is for you. I know this is your house…'

'Our house,' Dante corrected, but Matilda shook her head.

'It was yours and Jasmine's first so, please, don't try and tell me that you're not hurting, too.'

'A bit,' Dante admitted, gazing down at Joe, tracing his cheek with his finger, 'but I was giving Joe his bottle, thinking about our new home and Alex was running around, checking her dolls were all in her bag, laughing and talking, and I promise you, Matilda, all I felt was peace. I knew in my heart of hearts that Jasmine was happy for me, was finally able to admit...' He didn't finish but gave a tiny wry smile and attempted to change the subject, but Matilda was having none of it.

'Tell me, Dante,' she urged, because despite all the progress, despite their closeness, sometimes with Dante she had to. 'Please, tell me what you were thinking.'

'That I loved her.' He was watching her closely for her reaction, an apology on the tip of his tongue, but he held it back as she smiled. 'Is it OK to say that to you?'

'It's more than OK, Dante,' came Matilda's heartfelt answer. 'It's exactly how it should be.'

'I know we had our faults, I know that it probably wouldn't have worked, but sometimes when I see Alex laughing now, sometimes when she is being cheeky or funny, I can actually see Jasmine in her and finally I am able to remember the good bits. Finally I know that she is in a peaceful place. I know that she is proud of the choices I have made, and it's all because of you.'

She didn't even attempt to hide her tears, just leant on him as he spoke on.

'It's right to move on, right that we make a new start, with our little family.'

'But just because we're looking to the future, it

doesn't mean we have to shut out the past,' Matilda assured him. 'Even Katrina seems to have come around.'

She had. In the tumultuous weeks that had followed their revelation, it would have been so easy to hate her, but in the end Matilda had seen Katrina for what she was, a mother that was grieving, a mother terrified of the world moving on and leaving her daughter's memories behind. And slowly the tide had turned. Alex's stunning progress, Dante's respect, coupled with Matilda's patience, had won the coldest heart around.

'We need to do this,' Dante affirmed. 'We need to make new memories, build new gardens and look to the future…' He didn't finish, the words knocked from him as a very jealous young lady flung her arms around both of them, eyeing her new brother with blatant disapproval as she demanded to join in the cuddle.

'Together.' Matilda laughed, scooping up Alex, closing her eyes in bliss as the little girl rained kisses on her face. 'We'll do it together.'

REQUEST YOUR FREE BOOKS!

 HARLEQUIN® *Presents*®

2 FREE NOVELS PLUS 2
FREE GIFTS!

PASSION GUARANTEED SEDUCTION

YES! Please send me 2 FREE Harlequin Presents® novels and my 2 FREE gifts. After receiving them, if I don't wish to receive any more books, I can return the shipping statement marked "cancel." If I don't cancel, I will receive 6 brand-new novels every month and be billed just $3.80 per book in the U.S., or $4.47 per book in Canada, plus 25¢ shipping and handling per book and applicable taxes, if any*. That's a savings of close to 15% off the cover price! I understand that accepting the 2 free books and gifts places me under no obligation to buy anything. I can always return a shipment and cancel at any time. Even if I never buy another book from Harlequin, the two free books and gifts are mine to keep forever.

106 HDN EEXK   306 HDN EEXV

Name	(PLEASE PRINT)
Address	Apt. #
City	State/Prov. Zip/Postal Code

Signature (if under 18, a parent or guardian must sign)

Mail to the **Harlequin Reader Service®:**
IN U.S.A.: P.O. Box 1867, Buffalo, NY 14240-1867
IN CANADA: P.O. Box 609, Fort Erie, Ontario L2A 5X3

Not valid to current Harlequin Presents subscribers.

Want to try two free books from another line?
Call 1-800-873-8635 or visit www.morefreebooks.com.

* Terms and prices subject to change without notice. NY residents add applicable sales tax. Canadian residents will be charged applicable provincial taxes and GST. This offer is limited to one order per household. All orders subject to approval. Credit or debit balances in a customer's account(s) may be offset by any other outstanding balance owed by or to the customer. Please allow 4 to 6 weeks for delivery.

Your Privacy: Harlequin is committed to protecting your privacy. Our Privacy Policy is available online at www.eHarlequin.com or upon request from the Reader Service. From time to time we make our lists of customers available to reputable firms who may have a product or service of interest to you. If you would prefer we not share your name and address, please check here. ☐

HP07

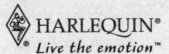

HARLEQUIN *Presents*

Proud and passionate...
Three billionaires are soon to discover
the truth to their ancestry.

*Though royalty is their destiny, these sheikhs
are as untamed as their homeland!*

**From the magnificent Blue Palace to the wild
plains of the desert, you'll be swept away as three
sheikh princes find their brides.**

THE SHEIKH'S
UNWILLING WIFE
by **Sharon Kendrick**

Five years ago Alexa walked out on her sham of a
marriage, but Giovanni is determined that Alexa should
resume her position as his wife. Though how will he
react when he discovers that he has a son?

On sale April 2007

They're tall, dark...and ready to marry!

If you love reading about our sensual Italian men, don't delay.
Look out for the next story in this great miniseries.
Coming soon in Harlequin Presents!

SICILIAN HUSBAND, BLACKMAILED BRIDE
by **Kate Walker**

Dark, proud and sinfully gorgeous,
Guido Corsentino must reclaim his wife.
But Amber ran away from him once,
and Guido resolves to protect her from the
consequences of her actions...in his bed!